Praise for Fairy Tale "" '

D1605835

"*Fairy Tale Wisdom* contains the personal reflect　　　　　　— ...
intelligent people on a few of the great stories. They put themselves into the
tales, or put the tales in them, and offer ways to both appreciate important
narratives and make sense of your life, especially as you grow older. I like
most the sincere probing that goes on in the reflections of these extraordinary authors."

　　　　　—Thomas Moore, author of *Care of the Soul* and *Soul Therapy*

"*Fairy Tale Wisdom* is a refreshing, new, and practical approach to tradition-
al stories for children. Now as elders, the authors return to the tales that
deeply affected them in childhood, from 'Little Red Riding Hood' to 'the
Prodigal Son,' and reflect on the evolving impact that the tales had on them.
Their comments move from personal history to the perennial questions that
inevitably arise, such as the meaning of tragedy and chance in life. Their
approach invites sharing with other people and would be invaluable in
seminars and workshops."

　　　　　—Allan Chinen, M.D., author of *In the Ever After*,
　　　　　Once Upon a Midlife, and *Beyond the Hero*

"This revelation of a book invites us to view the narratives that formed us
in childhood through the lens of maturity. What a pleasure to think with
these three old souls about how life has changed us and what matters to
us most now. An at once important and fun contribution to the conscious
aging genre."

　　　　　—Carol Orsborn, Ph.D., author of *The Making of an Old Soul*

"Fairy tales are for all of us. I am simply thrilled by your book and can't wait
to share some of the stories with our granddaughters. *Fairy Tale Wisdom* is
an indispensable contribution to this field of work."

　　—Harry (Rick) Moody, Ph. D., retired VP for Academic Affairs, AARP

"This unique and delightful book challenges the reader to pack a bag full of
familiar tales and plot lines and travel into the turbulent currents of time's
quaint stream. Reading it, I became an active traveler who, along with the

three writers, found myself navigating, reinterpreting and reimagining the intersections of stories and self over a lifetime. It's not a book that tells you how to achieve growth and wisdom through age but that brings you along for the ride."

—Kate de Medeiros, Ph.D., author of
Narrative Gerontology in Research and Practice

"After reading *Fairy Tale Wisdom*, I doubt you'll see your life or fairy tales in the same way again. Bill, Barbara and Andrew engage us in an abundantly creative journey back to the stories, fables and tales of our youth, inviting us to reexamine the unique meanings they can hold in later life. Coming from different personal and professional backgrounds, the authors' mutual love of and belief in the power of stories to enrich and shape our lives shines through every page. Deeply personal, illuminating the wisdom of each author as they reflect on their chosen tales, you'll find guideposts to help you mine your own stories and forge new directions on the inward adventure of aging. Poignant yet playful, this is a beautifully written, evocative book that you can and should pull from your shelf again and again. It is a wonderful meditation on the art of growing older and proof that fairy tales are truly for children of all ages!"

—Karen Skerrett, Ph.D., Psychologist, Consultant,
and author of *Growing Married*

"Like Bruno Bettelheim's *The Uses of Enchantment* and other notable forays into the world of make-believe, *Fairy Tale Wisdom* seeks to discern the meaning and significance of such fanciful stories for the lives of readers. In this case, though, the target readers are elders rather than children, and the purpose is nothing less than seeing in fairy tales, fables, and biblical parables an untapped source of wisdom about the 'adventure' of aging. An inspiring, fanciful, and most valuable new resource for exploring later life, *Fairy Tale Wisdom* is, in the authors' words, 'a way to the light' and thereby serves as an important counterweight to those images of darkness and decline that so often characterize the process of growing old."

—Mark Freeman, Ph.D., author of
Hindsight: The Promise and Peril of Looking Backward

"This delightful, creative book is both playful and deeply wise. It invites you to spend time in the company of three insightful older individuals who are imaginatively reconsidering the meanings of fairy tales and fables that they remember hearing as children. Together, they explore how the messages of these tales played out in their own lives and in their understanding of what it means to grow up and grow old. The authors regard aging as an intriguing adventure and a vantage point from which to think of one's life in its essential—and mythic—terms. Have you, for instance, been a tortoise or a hare? This book will invite you to consider your own life stories in new ways, much like an intense conversation with old friends."

—Ruthellen Josselson, Ph.D., author of *Narrative and Cultural Humility*

"This is a fascinating journey, through the lens of childhood fairy tales, from a soulful exploration of the authors' life stories, to the potential wisdom of later life."

—Gary Irwin-Kenyon, Ph.D., author of *Pathways to Stillness*

"Convene three septuagenarians, two of whom throughout their scholarly lives as gerontologists concerned themselves with the narrative self in the second half of a lifetime, who decide to revise some of the moral tales that informed their earlier lives, and you have an intriguing prospect. In the words of Nick Thompson, an Apache elder: 'This is what we know about our stories. They go to work on your mind and make you think about your life.' Nothing could more aptly describe how each author thinks about their lives from the perspective they share—their seniority. As a septuagenarian myself, their text guided me to similar ruminations."

—David Epston, co-author of *Reimagining Narrative
Therapy through Practice Stories* and *Autoethnography*

"*Fairy Tale Wisdom* is a generous invitation to reimagine many of the stories we heard growing up with a deeper, more contemplative posture. Randall, Lewis, and Achenbaum unveil their curiosities and interpretations surrounding these classic tales with vulnerability, grace, and humility. Simultaneously, they extend a gentle permission to the reader to consider their own lived experiences alongside the lessons hidden within these tales. I'm immensely grateful for the invitations, wisdom, and care the authors offer us in these pages as we each reflect upon these stories and navigate our own journey as a fellow traveler."

—Holly K. Oxhandler, Ph.D., LMSW, Associate Dean at Baylor University's Garland School of Social Work and author of *The Soul of the Helper*

"This extraordinary book is insightful, moving, full of wisdom, and amusing, all at the same time. Three masters of the human spirit and of words alike invite us to join their playful—yet extremely profound—inner adventure, demonstrating marvelously the inspirational power of stories in the never-ending process of growing old, rather than getting old."
—Gabriela Spector-Mersel, Ph.D., School of
Social Work, Sapir College, Israel

"This is a book for anyone who loves fairy tales and who wonders about how the stories we grow up with relate to the lives we live. Being led by consummate explorers of later life, the reader is guided through a range of imaginative tales, and along the journey examines ongoing layers of the meaning of life, nestled in our sense of who we are and who we are becoming."
—Molly Andrews, Ph.D., author of *Narrative Imagination and Everyday Life*

Fairy Tale
Wisdom

To Jen (and Susan)

With respect and
friendship.

Andy

Stories
for the
Second
Half
of Life

Fairy Tale
Wisdom

William L. Randall, Barbara Lewis,
and W. Andrew Achenbaum

For more information or to contact the authors, visit www.fairytalewisdom.com

The ideas and suggestions contained in this book are not intended as a substitute for consulting with a physician or professional therapist. Although the authors and publisher have made every effort to ensure that the information in this book was correct at press time, no liability is assumed for losses or damages due to the information provided. Readers are responsible for their own choices, actions, and results.

ISBN (paperback): 978-0-9736313-3-3
ISBN (ebook): 978-0-9736313-4-0

Copyeditor: David Hogan
Cover and interior design: Christy Day, Constellation Book Services
Publishing consultant: Martha Bullen, Bullen Publishing Services

Photo credits:
William Randall's author photo: Gary Weekes, Weekes Photography
Andy Achenbaum's author photo: Ayang Ayang
Barbara Lewis' author photo: Peggy Smith

Printed in the United States of America

To our parents—Bill and Emma, Ralph and Teddy,
Bill and Melo—with affection and respect

Contents

PART I

Once
Upon
A
Time

CHAPTER 1

The Inner Adventure of Later Life: An Introduction

Once upon a time, there were three septuagenarians who had so many interests in common and enjoyed each other's company so much that they decided they ought to write a book together. Not a textbook-y kind of book, like two of them (both gerontologists) had written too many of already, but a more personal kind of book. But not an autobiographical kind of book either, or at least not in a conventional sense, yet a book about themselves all the same, about their stories and about how those stories have changed over time—though in some ways have remained the same. So the three of them began chatting and chatting, and then chatted some more, occasionally in person but mostly through Skype, until, eventually, the book—this book, *our* book—came into being.

Our aim in it is to shed some much-needed light on the positive potential that's unique to later life, potential that, sadly, gets eclipsed by what seems society's preoccupation with aging's negative dimensions. Our aim, in other words, is to look at aging, despite the aches and pains, troubles and losses, that it can surely bring—in some

ways, *because* of these—as, at heart, not an unmitigated tragedy but
an intriguing adventure, a way to the light, you might say, and not
to the darkness alone.

Aging can be an adventure on several fronts of course as, for
instance, we take up a new hobby in retirement, or a new cause; as
we take a long-dreamed-of trip, or revive long-buried talents and
embark on exciting creative endeavors. It can be an adventure in an
interpersonal sense as we deepen existing relationships and forge
fresh ones as well—with grandchildren, for example, or with friends
we make in our travels but, earlier in life, would never have met. It is
an adventure, overall, as we widen our horizons in directions closed
off to us amid the hustle and bustle of our midlife years: raising
a family, pursuing a career, and keeping the wolf from the door.
Above all else, aging is an adventure inward. It is an adventure into
our souls, a journey into the wisdom that has accumulated quietly
within us across the years; an exploration into the mysteries and
ironies of our lives, the quirks and contradictions that run through
our nature and behavior, the open-ended issues or recurring themes
and the slow, persistent questions that time and circumstance have
seeded deep inside us.

We invite you to come with us on this adventure—this
autobiographical adventure—as we revisit an assortment of fairy
tales and fables, as well as parables and stories from the Bible, plus
other little narratives that we first heard or read so long ago but
that lodged themselves within our memories and have haunted us
ever since. As we've learned with a blend of delight and discomfort,
such stories can open up portals into our lives as aging individuals,
and indeed into aging in general, through which we can make out
patterns and possibilities that might otherwise have gone unnoticed,
and can come up against questions that might have gone unasked.
Each such question invites us on a *quest*, toward a broader, more
nuanced self-understanding, as we probe ever deeper the intricate

inner landscape that awaits us in the final chapters of our lives.

Given that the stories we're looking into are ones we've known for several years, it's been a fascinating, frequently surprising, experience to return to them in later life. While the origins of some of them—the tales of the Brothers Grimm, for instance, or the fables of Aesop, or stories from the Bible—are comparatively clear, and their versions quite consistent across the years, others have been handed down in collections of folklore that, over the centuries, have migrated from one culture to another, which means that they've admitted to a variety, not just of translations, but of tellings, too. What is more, we sometimes discovered elements within them that were decidedly different from our earlier recollections of them. Sometimes those recollections involved only a snippet of what was in fact a much longer story. Other times, details that we'd totally forgotten turned out to enrich immensely the meanings that the story can hold for us today. And, tomorrow, when we're eighty or ninety, what we get out of them could be a different story entirely! From each of these old tales, new meanings can always be gleaned. As such, there is no limit to how much they can assist us in truly growing old—not just *getting* old, for that's going to happen anyway, but consciously, intentionally *growing* old.

Overall, though, this book is not a scholarly endeavor, even if two of us (Andy and Bill) have been professors by trade and thus, here and there, cite the odd outside source. But it's far from being from an academic exegesis of arcane texts. Instead, it is a deeply personal, open-minded exploration of aspects of stories that, for whatever reasons, we've found meaningful for ourselves, and that hopefully you'll find meaningful as well. It is a respectful celebration of the gifts these little stories can still give us as we navigate the swirling, churning inner currents of the second half of life.

Occasionally, we found tales that spoke to all three of us, such as *The Tortoise and the Hare*, which we'll be looking at next chapter—even though each of us was working with a different version and, what is more, read it in rather different ways! But we also found stories that were, in fact, quite unfamiliar to one, or even two, of us. And just as the stories that spoke to us differed among us, so, too, have we taken different approaches and adopted different styles in responding to them. Which stands to reason, for we've inevitably interpreted them in terms of our own histories and personalities.

While, overall, our styles are more visceral, more live and un-plugged, than in the writing that each of us has done in the past, Bill's clearly leans toward the autobiographical. A former minister turned gerontologist, with a keen interest in the narrative com-plexity of later life (something he calls "narrative gerontology"), his voice is at once impish and bookish. Before retiring, Barbara was an Episcopal priest, and for twenty-five years before that, a practicing psychoanalyst in New York, a profession in which she asked a lot, a lot, of questions: *How did that feel? Why do you think that? What might that mean?* So her style, much more than Andy's or Bill's, tends toward the pastoral, the piercing, and the inquiring. As for Andy, Barbara's husband and, similar to Bill, a retired gerontologist, with a strong interest in the history of aging, as well as its spiritual dimensions, his style is witty, ironic, and wry. But whereas he and Bill are both inclined to turn inward and explore the terrain of their own life stories, Barbara reaches outward in a questioning, open-ended contemplation of the countless implications that a given tale can have for how *all* of us might think about our lives.

It's not just the style of our reflections that varies, however. It's our focus as well: what we each zero in on in the stories that we look into, whether it be their characters or plots, or certain images or themes, or how the stories as a whole have spurred us to re-in-terpret—to *re-member*—aspects of the stories of our own lives in a highly individual manner, thereby expanding the horizon of our self-understanding. It's our hope that the interplay among the three of us may lead to a comparable expansiveness in you. And "play" is the operative term, of course, for the chemistry we've enjoyed while working on this book, discussing our respective contributions, critiquing various drafts, has been nothing short of delightful, an adventure in friendship at its best. It's as if we've fed off of one another's thoughts and feelings amid our weekly meetings. As a result, each of us has grown inwardly in unforeseen ways.

These differences in style and focus have guided how we've sequenced the stories themselves, the ones that form the backbone of the book, in Part II. In other words, we've intentionally arranged them so that we go (as you might wish to, too, in reading them, though you certainly don't have to) from one by Barbara to one by Andy to one by Bill, being mindful in the process of varying the sources, and thus cultures, from which the stories hail—Grimm, Andersen, Aesop, the Bible, and the like. Arranging them according to theme, however—whether, say, love or hope, conflict or courage—proved impossible to do, as logical and sensible as that sort of system might seem. For we quickly found out that, once you look closely into it and ponder what it's in fact "about," each story is about several such themes at once, all of them—as with any great tale—hopelessly intertwined.

To give you a feel for how the three of us, and you yourselves, can draw quite different things from any given story, we've dedicated Chapter 2 to showing how each of us approached Aesop's famous fable, *The Tortoise and The Hare*. Later in the book, in Chapter 19, we offer a few further reflections on what we call the "parabolic power" that stories of every sort (life stories, too) potentially possess, while in Chapter 20 we provide practical strategies that you can use, and questions you can ask, in connecting stories to your own lives and thus finding new meanings in old tales. In between, from Chapters 3 through 18, or Part II, we tackle five or six tales apiece that, for reasons which will likely always be obscure, have stuck with us throughout our lives. Our hope is that our musings on them will trigger similar musings for you, or more likely, quite other musings besides. It matters not. In fact, they may trigger recollections of totally different stories altogether, stories which, like these little ones have done with us, have taken up residence in the secret corners of your heart. We invite you, then, to join us on this meandering adventure into the wonderland world which each such tale can be, in search of the treasure trove of wisdom that lies buried within it.

CHAPTER 2

The Tortoise and the Hare

BARBARA'S VERSION

The Hare was once boasting of her speed before the other animals. "I have never yet been beaten," said she, "when I put forth my full speed. I challenge any one here to race with me."

The Tortoise said quietly, "I accept your challenge." "That is a good joke," said the Hare; "I could dance round you all the way." "Keep your boasting till you've won," answered the Tortoise. "Shall we race?"

So a course was fixed and a start was made. The Hare darted almost out of sight at once, but soon stopped and, to show her contempt for the Tortoise, lay down to have a nap. The Tortoise plodded on and plodded on, and when the Hare awoke from her nap, she saw the Tortoise just near the winning-post and could not run up in time to save the race.

Then the Tortoise said: "Slow but steady progress wins the race."

I had always assumed that the "point" of Aesop's fables was the moral precept. Stories were appended, I thought, to make the axioms more easily recalled. But as I look at the story of the tortoise and the hare, it does not really seem to illustrate the importance of slowness and steadiness. It seems, in part, rather to point to the value of commitment and the importance of perseverance. Had Aesop wanted to illustrate the wisdom of approaching life (or its various component challenges) in a slow and steady way, he might better have told the story in a manner that did not focus on the hare's inattention to the goal, contempt for others, and general lassitude. In this story, it is the hare's essential refusal to race which determines the outcome, not the slowness and steadiness of the tortoise. One could imagine a story in which the hare strives with such overexertion that she collapses in exhaustion before reaching the goal; or in which she is so taken with the various styles of running that she gets caught up in fancy footwork and loses her way. Either of those approaches might make the point about the advantages of the tortoise's slowness and steadiness much more clearly. They would assert that it is the tortoise's virtues that win the race, rather than the hare's shortcomings.

Regardless of the "fit" between story and precept, however, perhaps we could look at the precept itself: "Slow and steady wins the race." On first reading (or remembering), this seems fairly straightforward. If we wonder at all, it may be at the fact that ancient Greeks had the same admiration for dogged perseverance that we do. We read it as exhorting us to plod along (some translations actually render the adage "Plodding wins the race"), doing the right thing, in the knowledge that we will be victorious in the end.

A few moments' thought, though, begins to be troubling. Is this motto true? What, in our culture, or to each of us, would "winning the race" entail? Might it be something akin to "success"? If so, are the most successful people you know (the "winners" of the world) plodders? If we see success in terms of money, fame, social status, or other quantifiable rankings, "plodders" do not seem to win the race. Standardized exams are timed. We are advised to "snatch the moment" lest the "right" time pass us by. Our culture certainly does not seem to prize steady, humble, protracted movement.

And what of the metaphor as a whole? Is life to be seen as a competition? As something we should try to "win"? It is certainly a widely-held approach. Sports metaphors abound and, in our highly capitalistic society, competition is a central reality—for social service agencies applying for relatively scarce charitable funds, as well as for corporations seeking to maximize shareholder returns. Certainly many of us have needed to hone our competitive gifts in order to make a living.

On the other hand, as we age, competition often seems to lose whatever luster it once had, if for no other reason than we are frequently bested by our younger competitors. We are "over the hill." We haven't become proficient in the new technologies used in our professional lives. Or, even if we've "kept up," the Young Turks are chomping at the bit, ready to take over the game. Ageism is rampant throughout most professions and industries, and even when we're confident that we haven't lost a step, our younger coworkers often seem eager to have us move on, even as they might praise us for what we have (had) to offer. This situation, of course, is all the more evident once we have actually retired. We might ask at any age—but may be required to ask as we get older—is a competitive, zero-sum view of the meaning of life useful to us?

Perhaps we might set aside the moral precept of Aesop's story and look primarily at the tale itself, without needing to find there a moral dictum. As it turns out, we have support for this approach. A number of scholars have suggested that Aesop's morals were later appended to the tales, and that Aesop hadn't actually written them at all, rather leaving the stories to speak for themselves. Although the tales were, especially after the advent of the printing press, frequently used in children's education, many believe that in the early days (after Aesop's life in the sixth or fifth century BCE) the fables were told to adults, and dealt with religious, social, and political themes. So they may well not have been initially focused on moral precepts, but on the pithy depiction of timeless human traits—without the added moral component.

Before the race begins, let's look for a moment at the onlookers. Who would be interested in watching such a lopsided contest? Are there some friends of Tortoise, maybe, who have told her there is no need to race? Who have reminded her of her many other gifts? Maybe some stay around for the race wanting to be there to console her after her loss. Maybe there are some who haven't thought about the disparity of gifts for the race, but just love to see the hare run—such a beautiful sight, with every muscle working as it should, propelling the animal in a graceful, lovely, moving picture. Are there, on the other hand, friends of Hare who are delighted with the idea of humiliating Tortoise? Unless they have prior reason to dislike her, might we imagine that such mean-spiritedness could reveal the painful insecurity of these viewers? Maybe there are some who want to bet on the race—focused not on the outcome itself, but on the margin of the win. For these, presumably, the race is not so much about their friends as about the excitement of betting itself and figuring out the odds. Tortoise and Hare have stopped being actual acquaintances, for these bettors, and become just a means to the excitement of the wager. It's interesting, perhaps, to think how easy it is to shift from thinking about real people—politicians, bosses, acquaintances, even close friends and family—and find ourselves viewing them as means to an end, focused primarily—or solely—on how their actions affect us. For the imagined bettors in this story, Tortoise and Hare are simply objects whose behavior will result in either the pain of material loss or the pleasure of its gain.

So we are ready for the race. First, Hare: she loses as a result of staggering hubris or an inability to maintain an enthusiastic sense of purpose. There are periodic stories of life's "winners"—"stars" whose names are familiar to the general public because of their success in some field—being brought down by revelations of personal or professional activities unsavory or illegal enough to deprive them of public adulation—or, in some cases, even employment altogether. In some ways, they might be compared to Hare in our fable, who treats the race (which she herself suggested) with arrogance and contempt for others, and despite her greater gifts, loses to the plodder. Cheers from the bystanders are heard throughout the media circus that ensues. The plodders can feel justified, and redeemed for their erstwhile failures, which are now seen as evidence of moral rectitude and true success. Perhaps this is our first emotional response to this story: *schadenfreude,* as we see the high and mighty fallen.

But such a current events analogy actually distorts the fable, whose quick-footed loser might be more complex than a simple narcissist who disdains the rules and finally gets caught. Our Hare plays by the rules, and wins almost all of her races because of her greater gifts. Her loss here is not due to moral turpitude but to loss of interest in the race. She has raced, very well, for long enough that others know that she's fast. She's right when she says that she could beat Tortoise even if her slower opponent ran as fast as she was able. Hare could prevail if she ran at half- or even quarter-speed, or simply walked. It's just that, at this point, she can no longer bear to put her energy into the race. She knows she can win; there is no challenge left in this arena. She has run the race, or others like it, for long enough, it seems, that the sense of challenge, the excitement of the contest, is no longer there. She can't make herself care, cannot commit herself to it. Maybe even worse, she no longer has respect for her opponents; she takes a nap in the midst of the race. To express her contempt for Tortoise? Or simply because she is too bored to retain even a modicum of energy for the race?

Is it possible that napping, or getting distracted from an assigned task, is—or can in some instances be—preferable to putting all your energies into an arbitrary competition? Is there any real inherent moral superiority in plodding on (especially, like the tortoise, competing in something which does not, apparently, utilize your real gifts, but highlights your limitations)? Is allowing yourself to be engaged/distracted by ostensibly valueless stimuli, activities, etc., necessarily bad? Is the value of napping absolutely less than that of running a race, or is the comparison a matter of cultural mores?

Maybe Hare has simply raced enough. Maybe she is only now beginning to see that she has achieved her life's work—has found her place in the competition with her peers, has proven her worth as a hare, and no longer needs to prove herself, to herself or to others. Perhaps her engagement in the race is her final undertaking—the one which makes her see how empty her racing life has become. She has done it: beaten creatures far faster than the tortoise, over and over again. Why continue with these races? What more does she need to prove? And to whom? Maybe it is time for her to rethink her priorities, and to give herself permission to take a break, to see that there are things in life that might, at this point, be more important for her than competition. It could be that there is something else in this world calling to her. Maybe she has gifts other than speed that are waiting to be used. Or maybe the invitation is simply to stop competing. Perhaps she has not spent enough time smelling the daisies, taking a nap, doing something that is not focused on competition with or for spectators, friends, bosses, or strangers, and it is time to expand her ideas about "worthwhile activities" and include things for which she would never get paid or be admired. Maybe it is time for her to think about retiring.

But Tortoise: why does she choose to compete? Maybe she is a sucker for lost causes—and is astonished when she wins. Maybe she has agreed to the race in an attempt, by giving her opponent one more victory, to curry favor with the quicker Hare, whose (apparently unavoidable) victory might result in future favors to the tortoise. Or she knows how much even such a ridiculously one-sided competition would mean to Hare and is willing to offer the Type A rabbit one more victory. Maybe Tortoise simply wants to give Hare something that seems important to her, at little cost to herself. So maybe the race is an act of generosity on Tortoise's part—a self-abasement in the service of adding to Hare's self-congratulation. Maybe she has lost races so often, been miserably defeated on such a regular basis, that she has come to see this as her destiny: merely the appropriate norm of her life. Perhaps she is so used to being a poor runner that she has lost sight of the gifts she does have, and settles for engaging in something for which she is particularly unfit. The lopsided loss would have highlighted Tortoise's inadequacy, and invited ridicule. At what point, then, might generosity of spirit become masochistic self-sacrifice? We may want to think about the balances we ourselves have made, and the possible self-sabotage that we have chosen to see as effusive generosity.

Let's, though, imagine a less sacrificial possibility for Tortoise. Something has led her to this seemingly assured loss. It is not as if she has no areas of strength herself. True, she also lags behind Hare in the prolific production of offspring. But she has other strengths, which seem potentially quite critical in their shared environment. She could certainly have won a contest requiring good armor against jaws, fangs, claws, traps, or snares—that shell is relatively impervious to attack, and it serves as a protective shield, enclosing legs, head, etc., so that nothing within it is harmed. She's good at camouflage, and is capable of silent stillness, eluding an attacker by seeming to be dead—or a rock. She's patient. But none of that is as visually impressive as running very, very fast. The finance consultant for the football team is not the one whose picture is in the paper every week, surrounded by adoring fans. Could Tortoise be unable to resist the fantasy of finally being the adored star?

Does she, perhaps, really think that she could win? Is this an instance of a stupefying lack of self-knowledge? Most of us have harbored, at some point or other, some fantasy about our gifts or capabilities that are unrealistic. We might have applied for—or even been given—a job for which we had every reason to know we were unprepared, but at which we would have loved to excel. Most have not had the fortunate result given to the tortoise in this story, but some of us do manage to hang onto the job and convince ourselves that the ability to put in the required hours somehow makes up for the lack of necessary talent. We may insist to ourselves that all that is needed is to be slow and steady (though coworkers and subordinates often suffer from our inadequacies), but we may suspect, in some uncomfortable corner of our hearts, that this is not a good fit in the first place, despite its perks.

As we age, we often come to a point in our career when continued advancement is clearly unattainable, and we can see the end of the employment journey. Sometimes, at such a point, we are able to look with greater clarity at what it is that we have brought to our career, and what gifts and abilities we have lacked along the way. Such an assessment may well allow us to recognize true gifts that we have either discredited or hidden from ourselves. For some of us, honest reappraisal may result in a recognition that our chosen career has never exercised our real talents. Perhaps one of the great gifts of later life is the freedom to leave a path that was never a good fit to begin with, and to seek other ways of using our time, talents, and energy more fruitfully. Or perhaps we have, in our career, used some of our gifts. It is possible—likely, perhaps—that other talents and interests have languished and not been developed.

If we can bear to see ourselves with such honesty, it may free us to look ahead with a clearer sense of our true gifts (and limitations), and thereby move into choices of how we spend our time and energy which more nearly align with our real interests and capacities, and develop long-ignored but potentially vital aspects of ourselves. We may never become another Bruce Springsteen, but we may truly enjoy taking up the guitar again, and entertaining not just ourselves but others.

ANDY'S VERSION

The hare laughed at the tortoise's feet but the tortoise declared, "I will beat you in a race!" The hare replied, "Those are just words. Race with me, and you'll see! Who will mark out the track and serve as our umpire?" "The fox," replied the tortoise, "since she is honest and highly intelligent." When the time for the race had been decided upon, the tortoise did not delay, but immediately took off down the race-course. The hare, however, lay down to take a nap, confident in the speed of his feet. Then, when the hare eventually made his way to the finish line, he found that the tortoise had already won. The story shows that many people have good natural abilities which are ruined by idleness; on the other hand, sobriety, zeal, and perseverance can prevail over indolence.

The tortoise does not always win, I painfully discovered. As a kid, I had terrible eyesight and tortoise-like feet—deficits that would hurt anyone eager to play sports. No matter how much I tried to make the line-up, I never was chosen to play third base. I was routinely picked after everyone else, and then consigned to *be* third base. How often I hoped against hope that somehow, someday, I would become someone endowed at birth with the gifts of a hare. Even mediocre fleet-footedness would have been good enough for me, hankering to be deemed second string. Yet I seemed destined to be the kid who could never persevere with enough zeal, extra-inning practices, prayers, or luck to make the team.

I was filled with remorse, as my friends (all of them, to my mind, all-stars) ran on to the field. I would shamefully eye my father, who was a gifted athlete, lower his head while watching me waddle back to the dugout. Although he never uttered a word about what he thought or felt, I could clearly see and remorsefully sense his acute disappointment. Looking back, I suspect that the really devastating judgment was self-inflicted. Surely not content to be a bystander, I came to loathe my bodily inadequacies. Drowning in self-pity, I was sure that I would never grow up to be an estimable man like Dad.

In 1950s America I had a happy childhood, despite finishing last every time I ran a half mile in gym. So this flat-footed tortoise sought success elsewhere—in books. Mom taught me how to read when I was four. Soon I was making weekly treks to the local library. Stumbling over polysyllabic words, I reckoned, induced less shame than my ghastly standing on the playground.

More savvy than gifted, I gradually realized that I did not need to be the brightest or most creative person in order to join the nerds' team. In fact, I managed quite effortlessly to shine as a student. In my plodding way, I met nearly every classroom challenge. I took advantage of all the help and advice I could get from peers and teachers. (Still trying to pay back those who convinced me that ideas mattered, I mentor friends and students stretching their imaginations.) College professors usually judged me a "competent" (alas, not "brilliant") undergraduate. Yet by the time I was pursuing a Ph.D., I staked out a niche that inspired my creativity and sparked generativity. I turned a 700-page dissertation (a history of old age in America) into a book that launched an academic career.

In my prime I stayed the course. I rarely relaxed, much less napped, on the job. Besides publishing a lot and winning teaching awards, I joined non-profit boards and civic organizations committed to enhancing the lives of older Americans. Capitalizing on seasoned tortoise-like skills, I became a full professor at a Big Ten university before I turned forty. Thanks to propitious timing and sure footing, I at last fulfilled my equivalent to a sandlot fantasy.

I was a respectable and respected hare—a minor-league player in a highly competitive academy. In due course I assumed administrative responsibilities, which I executed with mixed success. Duty bound to serve as a fox in an agonistic arena, I acted accordingly, and paid a price. I suffered a breakdown. That midlife crisis might have freed me to set my own course and the pace. Alas, old habits die hard. Back on the job, professional commitments and self-expectations trumped any incentive to explore other ways to run the race. That blind spot stunted me, delaying an imminent path to authenticity.

Focused on competing to win races, I ignored the meaning of the endgame. Failures tortured me in spiritual distress, which outweighed any satisfaction in successfully racing to perfection. Insecurities mounted in ceaseless struggles to persevere and thrive. Only now, in composing this reflection, do I honestly discern a striking disconnect between my life history and this fable's narrative.

My autobiography simply does not fit Aesop's moral about how and why that flatfooted tortoise bested the boastful hare. Is it because I survive in a world judged by intelligent and honest foxes and father figures? Dad died before I could redeem myself, professionally and personally, in his eyes. Yet was not the real competition within me? Why did I depend on approval from others, who had their own ups and downs? Why did I invariably don the hare's mask while speeding round and round the bases? Why was I not content to be a tortoise who, quite possibly, could anticipate a reasonably contented long life? Rarely did I sate my inner hare by indulging in a well-earned snooze. And I never could quite convince myself that the tortoise's shell might have made me less inclined to chew endlessly on shortcomings.

It took a long time for me to acknowledge opportunities to reconfigure how I understood the race. I did not have to be either a tortoise struggling with vulnerability or a boastful hare conforming to short-lived whims expressed by others. I had a chance to transform into an animal of my own making. After all, did not the fabled tortoise identify an "honest and highly intelligent" fox as another character?

Aesop suggests that the fox set the time and parameters of the race, but there is much more to be said. The fox in *The Tortoise and the Hare* is a bit player, a liminal figure probably known to be adaptable and resourceful. *That* fox does not resemble the protagonist in another of Aesop's fables. You know the one—the fox, who failing to leap high enough to reach the fruit of the vine, dismisses the lost prize as sour grapes. Foxes wear many masks.

And why not imagine characters off the race course? Another shamanic animal might suit me well. I could act like a hedgehog, intuitively following its natural curiosity. Maybe pretending to be a hedgehog would have given me the calmness I need(ed) to take care of myself. Does it matter that garlands await the tortoise or the hare who wins the race? What matters in real time is how individuals approach the finish line. Death, with no clock to beat, ultimately follows the cheering. All of us are runners in the race—a hedgehog, a fox, or maybe just a mortal human being who sits in the bleachers.

Life's successes and failures, which are always wrapped in fragility, ironies, and contingencies, characterize each runner and every race. Greek commentaries on Aesop summed it up by recommending *speude bradeos*, a phrase that Romans translated as *festina lente*. In plain English we say "make haste slowly" in order to see, hear, taste, and smell along the way.

BILL'S VERSION

A Hare one day ridiculed the short feet and slow pace of the Tortoise, who replied, laughing: "Though you be swift as the wind, I will beat you in a race." The Hare, believing the Tortoise's assertion to be simply impossible, assented to the proposal: and they agreed that the Fox should choose the course and fix the goal. On the day appointed for the race, the two started together. The Tortoise never for a moment stopped, but went on with a slow but steady pace straight to the end of the course. The Hare, lying down by the wayside, fell fast asleep. At last waking up, and moving as fast as he could, he saw the Tortoise had reached the goal, and was comfortably dozing after his fatigue. Slow but steady wins the race.

It's not much of a tale, as tales go. Little by way of complex plot, thickly drawn characters, and subtle, underlying themes. Here's basically what we have: Two animals compete in a race. The faster one is so confident of his abilities that he treats himself to a snooze halfway through. Meanwhile, the slower one—far slower one— keeps plodding and plodding until he passes his napping opponent and makes it to the finish line first. End of story.

An innocuous narrative, if ever there was one, yet it's one that I've never forgotten. I don't know where I first heard it or read it, but it's lodged itself into my memory ever since, worming its way inside my heart and powering my determination to keep on keeping on at every turn.

Truth be told, I've always thought myself a little on the slow side. I had a principal in my final year of high school who gave me the most back-handed compliment I think I've ever received. Referring to some student in the Grade 10 physics class that he taught, he said to me "She's really SMART!" "You're intelligent," he continued, in a conciliatory tone, as if awarding me the consolation prize, "but she's SMART!" I have colleagues on campus who are so smart, so good at cutting through wooly thinking and picking apart the logic of an argument, that I feel ... well ... *dumb* in their presence. I fumble in my thoughts, my tongue gets tied, and what tumbles from my mouth is stumbling and mumbling and thick. The same thing happens when I'm talking to politicians or university administrators or anyone I perceive to be in authority above me.

By this point in my life, of course, I realize that I'm smart enough, plus I'm intelligent to boot. And I've had accomplishments of which I'm rather proud, thank you very much. What is more, I've heard myself come out with puns at times that are up there with the best of them. Yet the feeling deep inside, deep down where stories take root and cast their spell upon us, is that I'm the tortoise, not the hare.

Much of this feeling, I've realized, is due to my dad. In the years leading up to his death at 98, he morphed, as many males can do, into the proverbial "sweet little old man" who, frail and weak, depended on me mightily for one thing or another every single day. But back when I was growing up, he was a force to be reckoned with ... and feared. Rooted in his own insecurities, I've since concluded, he had an annoying knack of making me feel totally incompetent. "Don't be so stupid," was a phrase he used a lot. Working with him on fix-it projects around our little hobby farm was therefore anything but fun, for if I failed to fetch the right tool in the right way at the right time, a sharp slap on the side of the head and a reminder to "SMARTEN UP" was not at all uncommon. And given his mercurial nature, you never knew when he would erupt again, so you were always on your guard. True, I managed later on to make it into Harvard, become a professor, publish a book or two, and fashion a respectable career—all of which has changed my mind a bit about my basic abilities. But in my heart, I'm still not all that swift.

Happily, however, "the race is not to the swift," or so the writer of Ecclesiastes claims. Which leads us to a few of the perils of swiftness . . .

Let's begin with basic biology. The swifter the species, the rapider its metabolic rate, and the sooner it burns out. The hurrier it goes, the behinder it gets. Hare today and gone tomorrow. It's said that the maximum life span for the European hare is five years, while the Galapagos tortoise can live to be a hundred. To the latter, the former is a flash in the pan.

When we're young, of course, flash is often what we prefer: the bright lights of the city, the glitter of celebrity, the stars who dazzle us with their looks and fame as they glow like gods upon the silver screen. With age, however, and having witnessed the rise and fall of more celebrities than we can possibly remember, our attraction to flash declines. And as our own powers themselves decline (our agility and mobility), we derive secret pleasure as yet another diva self-destructs or some bigwig in the world of politics or sports succumbs to temptation and ends up on the cover of the tabloids, their reputation ruined. Haughtiness and hubris, presumption and pride—all goeth before the fall.

As for the virtues of slowness, the older I get the more I appreciate how true it is that slow and steady wins the race. I think immediately of this guy I knew growing up. A couple of years ahead of me in school, he was the epitome of "cool," more mature in the ways of the world than I could ever hope to be. He smoked, he spat, he swore, and he pounded like a trucker down the hallways with clickers on his heels. As I slogged away each evening at my homework, he was cruising around the village, raising Cain. Far too smart (street-smart anyway) to be cooped up in a classroom, he quit school altogether and transferred out to the School of Hard Knocks. Last I heard of him, he had smoked and drunk himself into an early grave, while I kept slogging on. Now, here I am to tell the tale: Survival not of the smartest or the coolest but of those who stay the course. Then there are those dear, sweet souls who burst into your life, all bright-eyed and eager to assist, and assure you that they'll be there whenever they're needed. "Call me anytime," they fervently insist, and in the moment seem sincere. Then when you DO need them, there they are ... gone.

I've seen the same pattern with my students. While the brighter, quicker ones may shine in class discussions, they often fail to follow through. Classes get skipped and final assignments go unsubmitted. Meanwhile, the quieter, less flashy ones who come faithfully to class each week, hand their essays in on time, and generally do the best they can, end up getting their credits and, eventually, their degrees, and go on to do good things. To aid them on their path, I'm more than happy to write them letters of reference, or give them the benefit of the doubt when their grade is on the line and an extra percentage point could make the difference between a B and an A. It's the difference between fluid intelligence—how quick we can think—and crystallized intelligence, the knowledge we accumulate through education and experience. Of course, both would be wonderful to have, but at this point in my life it's substance that I'd opt for over speed.

As one who leans more to the humanities than the sciences, I see slowness as preferable to swiftness in the realm of knowledge in general. In saying this, though, I'm going against the grain. At a time when the humanities are scrambling to defend their corner of the academy, when what counts as knowledge in the first place is what can be transformed into a statistic and displayed on a graph, and when the quantity of your publications is valued above the quality of the thinking they contain, younger scholars are coached to ask only those questions whose answers can be calculated quickly and cranked out in an article. The deeper questions, the slower questions, the kind that have occupied philosophers for centuries and puzzled scientists at the frontiers of their fields (*Why is there Something and not Nothing? How did it all begin and where is it bound?*), take longer to ponder and seldom lead to easy answers.

Yes, I deeply respect the tortoise way. Indeed, I've lived my life by it in many respects, as well as the whole Horatio Alger script that I see it tying in with: the myth of Local Lad Makes Good, of the underdog who wins the day against all odds. In some secret corner of my soul, it's provided me with validation, infused me with moral support, and steeled my resolve to persevere at any task I undertake. And also, if I'm honest, to stay inside my shell, which calls to mind one of the earliest memories that I have of my life …

The year I turned two, I came down with polio—as did my two older sisters, Donna and Carol. Victims of an epidemic that struck thousands of children and adults alike in the early 1950s, we enjoyed the benefit neither of Medicare nor of the vaccine that has supposedly eradicated this scourge from the globe. Donna nearly died from paralysis of the trachea, while Carol, two years older, was rendered permanently disabled. As for me, the virus attacked my diaphragm, the muscle structure just below the lungs that, bellows-like, enables us to breathe.

For two weeks early on, so the story goes, I was consigned to an iron lung: a tank-shaped apparatus that assists our breathing from the outside. Without it, I would have died. With it, I lived to tell the tale. In that tale, I'm lying stoically inside it in a room that's barren and austere, not gaily papered with teddy bears and smiley faces like the average children's ward today. For my ordeal unfolded in an era when hospitals were less for getting well than for being ill. Outside the barred window of my solitary cell hangs the cold grey fog of Saint John, New Brunswick, on Canada's Bay of Fundy coast.

Dismal as it seems, I've always liked this little story, more just an image than a story really, but on scores of occasions I've recounted it to others. Often at parties, when the conversation turns to challenges that we've suffered and survived; occasions when a little sympathy can help you get your way. Frankly, I've liked how it portrays me, the vaguely flattering light in which my character is cast: a tiny child-hero who lies there and accepts his lot, imprisoned and alone, yet hero all the same.

The problem is: the story isn't true—or at least the part about the iron lung. It seems I got things wrong. According to my parents, whose recollections I finally ferreted out of them four decades after what I'd figured was the fact, it never took place. Oh sure, I had polio all right, and they were obviously concerned. Nor did they treat it lightly when later in the season I came down with pneumonia, which meant that I was placed in an oxygen tent and had my chest lathered with VapoRub. But that was apparently it. No iron lung at all. I'd trumped the whole thing up, they politely implied, cobbling it together from odds and sods of images and emotions, perhaps drawing on some photo of an iron lung that I'd seen one time in a magazine. With equal politeness, I implied that they had done the same with *their* version, and that being my parents didn't automatically place them nearer the truth. In fact, The Truth, I gently suggested, had had to be doctored because it was too hard to handle—that they had been powerless to care for me; that in my darkest hour, they'd abandoned me to a machine.

In the end, of course, I had to concede that they were right and I was wrong. But the story, I've come to see, is still "true." Like a tortoise in its shell, I'm still the lad inside the iron lung. While, yes, I can read it as a tale of my stick-to-it-iveness, of my ability (more or less) to deal with whatever fate places in my path, I've always been something of a loner, and I've known my share of confinement.

For starters, I frequently played by myself as a child. A natural introvert and a preacher's kid to boot, with loads of chores to do each day after school, I seldom hung out with the kids in the village where we lived. My father wouldn't have approved. Later, at college in the late sixties and early seventies, I was even less of a social butterfly, with only a few close friends. And I had even fewer when I took refuge in the more fundamentalist faction of the Harvard-Radcliffe Christian Fellowship. This in turn, though it helped to hold me together while anti-war marches and student strikes were keeping campus life in general disarray, became a prison of its own. It certainly filled my head with a host of theological hang-ups that it's taken decades to leech from my system.

After graduation, I spent another half-decade preparing myself for ministry, an all-consuming vocation in which the needs of others get put before your own, at that very stage in my development when I ought to have been nurturing relationships with possible mates. Instead, *married to the church*, as the saying goes, I was assigned to serve five tiny hamlets on the prairies of southwestern Saskatchewan, 120 miles from the nearest city of any size, with scant chance to socialize with anyone other than my parishioners. Three years later, I went on to spend a further six years ministering to a congregation in the city where I live at present, where the pool of potential partners was far greater, to be sure, but my freedom to swim in it felt no less restricted, given the on-call nature of my life and the public profile of my role.

As it's turned out, much of my life since leaving the ministry and becoming an academic has had its own constraints as well, for it's largely been taken up with writing books. While writing is an eminently rewarding endeavor, it's eminently solitary too. And it typically confines you to what's happening in your head. At the same time, the theme that runs through all these books has been the role of narrative in shaping our lives from beginning to end. It's as if sixty-odd years later, my story of the iron lung—above all, the version I have of it now, in which I'm *out* of the iron lung—has morphed into a story about the peculiar importance of stories themselves: about how we adopt them and adapt them for all manner of reasons, how they host all sorts of metaphors and themes that we can end up taking to heart, and how, largely unwittingly, for better or for worse, we live our lives in terms of them.

Meanwhile, back at *The Tortoise and The Hare*, it's the former, as I say, with which I identify more readily. And yet …and yet … there's this teensy-weensy part of me that sympathizes with the hare. When you think about it, he wasn't all that bad, just being true to his nature and doing what it is that rabbits do best, namely hop around a lot. As we grow older, this fuzzying of issues is precisely what takes place. Less and less, do we see the world in terms of black and white, good and bad, right and wrong, for the boundaries are increasingly blurred. *Postformal thinking* is the fancy term that gerontologists use, its hallmarks being a tolerance for ambiguity, a capacity for seeing different sides of any situation, and an openness to the meanings that myths and metaphors—even fables, too—can hold for us as we employ them to help us make sense of our lives.

It's why, for some ironic reason, the hare has been connected in my head with Wile E. Coyote, that classic cartoon chump, that underdog par excellence, whom Roadrunner (meep! meep!) is forever outfoxing. It's the bird (quick and speedy) that wins every time, and in that sense parallels the tortoise (slow and steady). But it's poor old Wile E. to whom my heart goes out. It's complicated, in that special way that stories often are. For one story leads to another, and another, and another, until their plotlines overlap and their characters converge to the point where it's impossible to say where one begins and another one ends. Is the tortoise, I ask myself, the counterpart in my imagination to Roadrunner—since both of them are winners—while the hare is the counterpart to poor old Wile E., the one I pity more? I could continue, of course, and drag in a link to Tweety and Sylvester as well, or even Bugs Bunny and Elmer Fudd. But let me take the high road instead and say that it's the same complication that makes me empathetic toward the older brother in the one about the prodigal son, which I'll be pondering later in this book.

I realize that *The Prodigal Son* is supposed to be a parable of the Kingdom, of how Grace cannot be earned by works but can only be received by faith, but I've always felt that the situation it describes simply isn't fair. The younger son leaves home and squanders his inheritance in riotous living and finally ends up eating with the pigs. Then, he has this grand epiphany, realizes the error of his ways, and comes crawling back to dear old Dad, who welcomes him with open arms and throws a banquet in his honor, replete with fatted calf. Meanwhile, his far-from-flashy sober sibling, who's remained behind and labored on the family farm, honoring his parents and carrying out their bidding, seems taken for granted. It's he who does the work, yet his wastrel of a brother is the one who wins the father's heart.

It's as if the hare is the winner after all. So, then, I'm back to sympathizing with the tortoise, and to how slow and steady wins the race, or ought to, if in this case it does not.

There's a lot of the older brother in me, you see; the secret complainer who feels that, in many ways, he's put his life on hold in the service of something else: his studies, his students, his parishioners, and most recently his aging parents. I'm the archetypal Good Little Boy, who followed in his father's footsteps (leastwise for a while), and now at seventy find myself wondering at times where my life has gone, wishing I'd been more daring in my younger years, more riotous all around, not played it so safe. Wishing I had stuck my neck out more.

Tortoises are notoriously self-protective, scarcely famous for their pluck. The minute there's a hint of trouble, they retreat inside their shell. On the other hand, they're notoriously determined too. (Q: *Why did the turtle cross the road?* A: *To get to the other side.*) Come hell or high water, they make it to their destination—a quality I feel

I've had in spades throughout my life. Rooted in a sense of duty, of conscientious guilt, or of "there but for the Grace of God go I," there's this doggedness, this drivenness, about me. Maybe it's a form of OCD for which I ought to have been treated long ago, but if I say that I'm going to do something, be it keep myself fit, care for my parents, or publish a book, then by golly I'll do it. And yet ... and yet ... like the hare, I too have slept on the job a time or two, squandered an opportunity once or twice, missed a deadline here and there, and not always stayed the course. Not to mention had my share of hare-brained ideas. And more than once—in the lottery of Love, to take one example—I've had my share of losses.

The story ends by spelling out the moral that we're meant to take away from it, in case there's any doubt: *slow but steady wins the race.* Straightforward and to the point. What more is there to say? Yet as tidy as this ending sounds, the story as a whole refuses to conclude, for it stirs up questions that keep rumbling through my mind, one question above all: Am I the tortoise or the hare? Or perhaps a bit of both? Perhaps I'm the tortoise in hare's clothing, or just possibly the other way around: the hare inside his shell.

CODA

As the three of us harken back to childhood memories to reflect on Aesop's famous fable, our interpretations share a lot in common. We revisit it with fresh eyes, seeing facets of our pasts as if for the first time—ones that reconfigure patterns for us while, at the same time, emboldening our futures. It stirs up mature and wondrous discoveries for each of us, as we hope it might for you, leading you to new adventures as you journey deeper into the second half of your life, too.

Somehow (and it really doesn't matter how) *The Tortoise and the Hare* still speaks to us. In our respective contributions to this chapter, in other words, we've each used it to filter recollections of experiences and relationships that mattered to us *once upon a time*. In the process, though, it has enlivened insights into the transitions that growing older may hold in store for us in the future as well. And it has encouraged us to ask ourselves questions—lots of questions—that we have shared with one another freely.

Some questions were straightforward, such as how to deal with the significance and inconsequence of "competition?" Other questions arose contemplatively. Still others pierced viscerally. Was there really any "right" answer or "best" approach to analyzing Aesop's cast of characters? Certainly not, we concluded. Far from being one-dimensional beings, the tortoise, the hare, and the other animals think precious thoughts and feelings. Just as we reflect appreciatively and provisionally on the various creatures' complexities and contrarieties, so we invite you to do the same!

We've obviously related to the same story in quite dissimilar ways, indeed relying on different versions of the fable itself! Might this have affected how we proceed? Perhaps, but probably not: From the get-go, the three of us run on different tracks. Has a course on socio-biology at Harvard prompted Bill to size up the tortoise's feet and comment on mammals' comparative longevity? Andy's foot fetish often animates his interpretation of the story, while Barbara digs in her heels, apparently having no footloose interest in whether size matters. In short, as we re-read and ponder what to take away from Aesop's famous tale, we embark on distinctive self-reflexive adventures.

Our respective renditions of *The Tortoise and the Hare* invite you to embrace divergent, highly personal perspectives from the ones that we've presented here. Far from competing with one another, each of us runs with the tortoise and tarries with the hare, while watching the race along with the fox and other bystanders. In other words, we are free to let our imaginations soar, because there is no *single* way to interpret this or any other story. This open-ended tack frees you, too, to craft your own interpretations as you model our complementary, disjointed styles.

Barbara asks questions, lots of questions, which frame boundless possibilities for interpreting the tale. Why, she asks, is there a race in the first place? Can Aesop's moral precept be taken off the track? Do onlookers thrill to the sport? Are they to cheer on their friend (the winner) and show contempt for the loser? Or does their presence (wonders Barbara in her surprising twist of the narrative) "point to the value of commitment and the importance of perseverance?" And what characterizes the relationship between the tortoise and the hare, both *females* in her interpretation? Is the former, bound to lose once again, trying to curry the latter's favor in "masochistic self-sacrifice?" Or, acknowledging unfitness and then winning an unexpected victory, is the slow-footed one at last free to race to strengths, pursuing talents that give her pleasure?

Barbara's queries are powerfully provocative. And they serve a purpose: she focuses on the small details to illuminate the big picture. That she listens attentively may attest to her years of being a psychoanalyst, pastor, and spiritual director. Her questions reveal a fierce desire to meditate on possibilities that might unfold in the present moment. Her tack, rarely self-disclosing, permits her readers to compose their own stories on an uncluttered canvas.

Andy goes to an almost opposite extreme. Unlike Barbara, he asks few questions. He shares painful revelations, fretfully mindful that a prime-life breakdown shattered his mask and allowed shadows to surface. It takes artful work for him to expose his butt while straddling the fence. Looking back, he realizes that he's grown comfortable living in the margins; that liminality has proven advantageous. The pattern began with cheekily competing with a father adept at masking his own dark feelings.

Throughout his account, Andy plods along. He figures out how to play to strengths on a highly competitive academic track. He soldiers on professionally, deploying strategies for obsequiousness and shrewdness he had honed at home. Approaching the finish line, he is neither tortoise nor hare. Instead, he identifies with the fox, wondering whether he really were a hedgehog. His rendition ends plausibly, without demanding closure. This playful process permits you to do the same. The three of us encourage you to place off-the-track bets—if and when you so desire.

Real-life experiences and references to popular culture inform Bill's interpretation. Having survived polio in an iron lung (real or imagined), he lives to retell the tale over the course of his life. "Frankly, I've always liked how it portrays me, the vaguely flattering light in which my character is cast: a tiny child-hero who lies there and accepts his lot, imprisoned and alone."

Bill goes on to re-present himself as a son ineptly trying to please a charismatic, larger-than-life father while they worked together on the family farm. Later on, in school and in the ministry, he wistfully wonders what would have happened if he had been "cool"—quickly adding concerns that feigning awesomeness would undermine an authentically modest persona. Lancing regrets with grace, humor, and bad puns, he alludes to Horatio Alger, Bugs Bunny and Elmer Fudd, Tweety and Sylvester, and Wile E. Coyote and the Road Runner. Bill, it turns out, actually, is quite content with being a hare observing life inside a tortoise shell. But it's not the end of his story.

The Tortoise and the Hare lodged in his memory and encamped in his heart. Ironically, though, he turns the tale on its head, immersing himself in what really matters. "An innocuous narrative, if ever there was one, yet it's one that I've never forgotten," he writes. "It's not much of a tale, as tales go. Little by way of complex plot, thickly-drawn characters, and subtle, underlying themes." Admitting some sympathy with the hare, however, he finds that the narrative lines have become fuzzy for him over time—as with many other life moments he re-stories. Aesop's fable is a story that, "as a whole, refuses to conclude, for it stirs up questions that keep rumbling through my mind." How conjoined to Barbara and Andy he sounds!

We re-compose from late-life vantage points a fable first heard as children. Interpreting it very distinctively, each of us inserts hunches and raises questions that, advertently and inadvertently alike, lie hidden between the lines. We are playful in rendering our various responses to it—as we will be doing, too, with the tales we turn to now. And we hope that you will do the same. Feel free to do what you like. Listen to your own voices, be they loud, dissonant, or muted. Don't be afraid to uncover serendipitous insights as you ruminate upon these little stories. How do you recall them? What meanings have accrued for you around them as you've gotten older? In what way does re-reading them help you to imagine your future selves?

We want you to discover meanings on your own. Permit yourself to explore what each story at the center of this book prompts you to re-member and the thoughts and feelings it stirs up. Maybe it will evoke hopes and hurts, fantasies and fears, that have been running through your hearts since childhood. Maybe it will shine glimmers of truth into your inner world and disclose things about yourself that you previously haven't understood, let alone noticed. Of course, if a particular story (and our reflections on it) doesn't especially speak to you, then set it aside and move on to the next. Only you can discern and decide which messages you encounter in which stories are meaningful for you. Overall, however, our hope is that in reading *Fairy Tale Wisdom* you will experience similar adventures to those that we've experienced, wide-ranging in nature and brimming with intriguing self-discoveries.

PART II

Re-Membering Stories

CHAPTER 3

Little Red Riding Hood

BARBARA

Once there was a girl named Little Red Riding Hood. The nickname came from the red hooded cape that she wore, given to her by her beloved grandmother, who lived not far from the girl and her parents, in a house in the nearby woods.

One day, the grandmother fell ill, and the family wanted to check on her and to make sure she was fed and getting better. Little Red Riding Hood's mother felt the girl was now old enough to go by herself; she warned her not to linger, but to go straight to the ailing woman's home. Little Red Riding Hood, though, was delighted by the flowers and woods, and was happy to talk to a friendly wolf who approached her.

The wolf was, in fact, up to no good, and when Little Red Riding Hood told him about her ailing grandmother, he encouraged her to linger and pick some flowers as a present for her grandmother. While she did so, he went to the grandmother's house and gained entry by pretending to be Little Red Riding Hood. He swallowed the grandmother whole, disguised himself in her clothing, hopped into her bed, and waited for the girl.

When the girl arrived, she noticed that her grandmother looked rather strange; when the woman talked, the voice was off, too. Little Red Riding Hood said, "What a deep voice you have!" "The better to greet you with," responded the wolf. Little Red Riding Hood was a bit confused. "Goodness, what big eyes you have!" she said. "The better to see you with," the wolf answered. "And what big hands you have!" "The better to embrace you with," responded the wolf. Still confused, Little Red Riding Hood said, "What a big mouth you have!" "The better to eat you with!" responded the wolf, at which point he jumped out of the bed and ate the little girl. Satiated, he immediately fell asleep.

We can all imagine—or remember—the horrified shock of the child hearing this story: "The better to *eat* you with!" And our heroine is summarily eaten. The tale, it is said, was told as a cautionary story to teach children not to dawdle or get distracted but to focus on a given task. Surely good advice for "getting ahead" in the world, advice that many of us heard frequently enough to make it a life precept. It may, in fact, have made it possible to succeed at difficult but worthy tasks, to learn meaningful information and skills. If we've followed the counsel to keep our noses to the grindstone, and found it essential advice to making a living and attending to life's necessities, we may want to congratulate the storyteller on helping children learn to focus and do what they are told. Good advice, perhaps. But in the story, Little Red Riding Hood is *killed* because she dawdled, thereby giving the wolf time to eat and take the place of the grandmother. Kind of a rough lesson.

Many people will note the ameliorating coda to the story supplied by later writers, from the Grimm brothers to Walt Disney: the wolf is killed by a fortuitously passing woodsman; both Little Red Riding Hood and her grandmother pop out of the wolf's stomach—alive, unchewed and still fully clothed, apparently. But it is not this soothing, sanitized ending which seems to be the centerpiece of most recollections. What children—and adults—recall most vividly is "the better to eat you with" and the subsequent attack on our little heroine.

We might wonder just who the later sanitizers were protecting—and who it was who needed the bowdlerization: the children nestled in familial laps, enjoying the thrill of pretending; or the adult storytellers, fully aware of the multitude of real-life dangers that threatened both themselves and their children? To most children, it is a story with a frisson of immediately conquered fear. Adults, though, know that children—and they themselves—*can* be killed by any number of actual threats to existence. Grown-ups may struggle between a desire to encourage children's fantasies, protecting them from life's dangers, on the one hand, and, on the other, teaching them to protect themselves by telling them the frightening truths about the big bad world.

What of our own caretakers? Were we left too much to fend for ourselves? Or wrapped too tightly in swaddling clothes that hampered our belief in our own independent capacities? At some point, like Little Red Riding Hood, we probably took off through the unfamiliar woods, heading toward the city, the university, the country, or the career where we hoped to meet people more like us than those at home, where we would study things more fascinating than what we'd already learned, in a beautiful new place filled with better versions of our favorite things. We would head toward our grandmother, the best of everything we love; on the way, we might stop and explore, and might find things we're eager to experience, which will make our life, and the lives of those we love, richer.

But Little Red Riding Hood stops to smell—and pick—the flowers, and is killed. This seems rather cruel, particularly since the flower-smelling is in the service of finding a gift for her grandmother.

Maybe the sin for which she is punished is not her distractedness from the task but her attention to a stranger, and trusting his tempting advice rather than following her mother's dictates. Perhaps the issue is one of Little Red Riding Hood's movement toward independence.

How have we "followed the rules"? Some of us, throughout our lives, have been the "good children": doing what is expected, following orders, hewing the well-trod path. Maybe we have been too willing to deny our own interests and needs, so as to please other people. Or perhaps we have been rebels, forging our own paths, breaking rules that intruded on our own desires. Maybe we have insisted so much on doing our own thing—whether that be rigidly following rules or flouting them—that we have been unwilling to take other people's needs and desires sufficiently into account. Is this a question just about rules, or it is also an issue of balancing our own needs and desires against those of others? Have we found an equilibrium—and relationships—which satisfy?

And what of our treatment of those in our care? Perhaps we have been overprotective. Or maybe we allowed the children in our care to come too close to dangers we might have mitigated. Little Red Riding Hood's mother is a relatively shadowy figure, whose only role here is to admonish her child not to loiter on the way to grandmother's house. She seems to be a caring person who is trying to help her daughter as she grows into responsible adulthood. Knowing of the loving relationship between girl and grandmother, the mother facilitates and seeks to strengthen the relationship. The girl, like probably every reader of the story, takes her mother's admonitions with a grain of salt, and easily finds a way to rationalize dallying amid the flowers. We may imagine the horror as the mother hears of her daughter's and her own mother's deaths at the hands of the wolf. She might blame the wayward daughter; or flagellate herself for inadequately protecting the girl. As we try to guide our children toward adulthood, how many mistakes have we made? Some parents have a tendency toward overprotectiveness, and some toward being too unstructured. Every one of us, as a parent or guardian or caretaker with any self-awareness and honesty, can recall ways in which we misled our children, made mistakes, and either stifled their growth or put them in undue danger—or both, at different times. A combination of acknowledging mistakes and finding a way to forgive ourselves for them can lead to an acceptance of the reality that neither we, nor the children, were ever perfect.

As we age, of course, younger generations grow to adolescence and adulthood, and become poised, eager, and sometimes insistent on taking over the responsibilities of adulthood. Some older people—more women than men, and more baby boomers than subsequent generations—have stayed home, raising children and/or providing a retreat, as pleasant as possible, from the demands of the world. If we have raised children, our own aging corresponds with the aging of our children and the length of our tenure depends, to a large extent, on the age(s) of our offspring. Very often, they leave home once they reach adulthood, as Little Red Riding Hood appears to have done.

Adult familial relationships usually do not have predetermined cancellation dates. If you have worked outside the home in some paid or unpaid job or career, however, you may well be expected to retire at a certain point. You may, over the years, have moved from peer/colleague to authority figure/teacher, perhaps ending happily as admired elder—or unhappily as either an esteemed but unnecessary old-timer or an unwanted hanger-on. It is clear that our own fears and anxieties may make it difficult to discern how our fellow workers view us. It is also likely that we ourselves are ambivalent about what we want to do with our gifts, our knowledge, and our experience. We may wonder about our interests and the numerous "paths not taken," which might yet be further explored if the time spent on our career is lessened. At some point—even if only when we die—we will stop working.

Some have the option of continuing to work part-time. For some, full retirement is required. Familial responsibilities may have been significantly lessened, with children having grown. If you plan to—or must—retire fully, there may be ways you can continue to use your gifts: as a volunteer somewhere, or as a freelancer of some sort. Some want to continue in their field of work. Others may choose to learn another skill, like ballroom dancing or playing the guitar, or to explore a different field of study, or teach newcomers, or work with the underprivileged, or volunteer in some other way instead. Some want to bask in the freedom of *not* being productive, and are eager to relax and read solely for enjoyment, or do a jigsaw puzzle. It may be helpful to think about what you "owe" others, and how to balance that against what you yourself want to do.

The "middle generation"—parents of children still needing care who are also children of parents now needing care—face significant challenges. But challenges as we move into the oldest generation are often equally complex—just different.

Although we actually never meet her, it is the grandmother's loving relationship with her granddaughter that is both causative of and central to the story. She has lovingly tended to Little Red Riding Hood in past days, notably by making the striking cape worn by the girl. Now, though, the older woman is ill, and it is the granddaughter who tends to her. Little Red Riding Hood is perhaps still less than an ideal caretaker, allowing herself to be distracted by her generous instincts to give her grandmother a bouquet. But she is feeding the ill woman; their positions have been somewhat reversed from prior days, one imagines. Maybe the grandmother has been suffering from a temporary illness. But, sooner or later, the old woman may become terminally ill and the role reversal will last until her death.

I wonder how the grandmother feels about it all. Does she enjoy the grand-maternal role? Her making of the cape may suggest a personal gratification which goes beyond the required duties. Is she content, after her years of raising at least one child, and clearly having been involved in the care of at least this one grandchild? Is she ready to cede the caretaking role to the new generation?

The grandmother seems fortunate in her familial relationships, and she maintains close ties with her granddaughter and, we assume, the girl's parents. She seems to have maintained her own independent household, and perhaps the illness at the time of the story would be cured (were it not for the wolf!). At some point, though, her independence would likely become compromised by failing health, and her days as cape-maker would give way to a period, of whatever length, of invalidism and dependency. Might she have to move into her daughter and son-in-law's cottage? Might we, in similar circumstances, face a move to a child's home or a long-term care facility? Our familial relationships change as we, and any children we have, age. Older people, and their children, often struggle with the shifts in these relationships, and with the changes that require shifts in roles and responsibilities. We may face further limits of choice because of our health or finances. It may be useful to acknowledge both our limitations and the fear, anger, and other emotions that result. Doing so may not "fix" things, but can serve to encourage us to find ways—including, maybe, psychological, medical, spiritual, or other resources—to help handle the changes.

The role of the wolf, of course, is the hinge on which the entire story turns. The idea that Little Red Riding Hood's growing independence may be at issue coincides with a current theme in commentary on this story: the idea that the wolf can be seen as a sexual predator, who rapes the girl. In this view, the wolf stalks her in the woods and charms her by suggesting she find flowers to give her grandmother, whom he then impersonates. She is a bit leery but he seduces her with his quick answers to her minimal wariness. Then, having succeeded in getting her close enough, he suddenly, without warning, grabs her—and takes her.

This approach to the story may invite you to think about your own initiation into sex and your views of sexual relationships. Were you pressured—by our culture, by another person—into sex too early? Did you put it off too long? Was your first partner someone you chose, or was she or he chosen for you? Do you regret your initiation into sex, and if so, whom do you hold responsible? Have you ever been coerced into intercourse? By society, family, your sexual partner? Have you, on the other hand, been wolf-like? Have you ever pressured someone else into sex, perhaps trying to convince yourself it was what the other "really wanted" despite protests to the contrary? Have you ever offended others by words or actions that they indicated they found intrusive or sexually demeaning?

It feels to many as if the rules regarding all of this have changed suddenly—or at least over the course of our own life-times. Many people have reconsidered their own sexual history in the light of these changes. Some, particularly women, have been reassured and healed by reinterpretations of sexual mores. Many men have re-examined their—and their fraternity brothers', teammates', colleagues', bosses', or other friends'—attitudes toward women and sex, and have found them, in retrospect, in need of reform. What is your sexuality like today? Was sex always—or has it become—a means of expressing deep connection with another human being? Do you see—have you experienced—sex as a gift of love?

Sex is only one of the complicated realities to which growing up exposes us. The wolf may personify any of multiple dangers of the world that we encounter as we leave home and grow up: for example, the world of work, travel, or higher education. We can be ensnared by any of these, led into dangerous new terrain. Often, young people leave home looking for something new, yet familiar:

sometimes, the adventure we embark on seems to have a connection to something we know—to be a bigger, better version of something familiar that we love. Some eagerly seek something totally different. We may want to think about how we found "the world" once we left home.

When we left childhood to become adults, we may have done so in innumerable ways. We may have stayed at home, taking on increasing responsibilities, including getting a job. We might have moved into our own home in the same town in which we were raised. We might have left home to live and work elsewhere. We might have left to go off to school and then made our own home apart from our parents and the rest of our family. Regardless of how we did it, we left off being a child and became an adult. Did our idea of the unknown change after we began to encounter it on our own?

There is a human tendency to fear the unknown; there is another tendency to assume that the future holds nothing but lovely surprises. When we are moving into a slightly different version of what we know (down the street, or to a school where most people will be like ourselves, or to a job which we could do with our eyes closed), we are able to imagine a lovely world with all that we enjoy, but with none of the disadvantages of our current situation. The more unfamiliar the new situation is, the more we tend to be fearful, unsure that we will know how to manage. Whatever exciting or terrifying fantasies of the world we may have harbored, we will at one or more points have been knocked down. We may even have felt destroyed. But, one way or another, we have managed to stand up again and keep going, very often with an increasingly realistic view of what might be ahead. There may well have been ways in which things about which we had been warned turned into delightful, novel experiences. Most likely, we have become able, often, to manage our fears, overcome our hesitancies, and come to revel in the novelty we discovered after we left home and became independent adults.

One final thought …

The wolf seems to represent all that is different and unknown. We fear we will be killed; we will end up in the belly of the wolf. We have no idea what this will be like, except that it will take us from everything we have ever known, and so it is terrifying to face the hungry beast. But if we see it as the embodiment of our greatest fear—of death—we may want to take a second look. What if being eaten by the wolf is not the end of all good, but the beginning of all that is best? If we remove our assumptions of his evil, we may find him inviting, doing his best to appease our fears. His deep voice is to greet us, his eyes are to see us afresh, his hands to embrace us. Even his desire to eat us can be heard as a desire to take us into himself as deeply as possible. Might this not lead us to a frightening wolf trying to find ways of assuring us that his desire for union with us is, in fact, a sacred one? An invitation to a deeper existence? Is not the holy always initially frightening in its power and strangeness? And so we will die. But perhaps we will smell the flowers, pick the daisies, dance through the woods, and join, in some mysterious, exhilarating way, our beloved grandmother, changed and yet familiar.

CHAPTER 4

The Fisherman and His Wife

ANDY

One day, after a poor man catches a flounder that begs to have its life spared, his spouse seizes on a way to improve her lot in life. Sensing that the fish has magical powers, she insists that her husband return to the shore to ask for something in return. After the fish grants the request to upgrade the couple's hut, the pattern repeats. After the fish honors the wife's mounting desires for power and wealth, the spousal demands prove excessive; the fish sends the poor fisherman back home to a hovel.

This summary of *The Fisherman and His Wife* does not capture rich details in the Grimm brothers' tale about an impoverished couple who live in a seaside shack. After the husband catches a flounder, which begs to be set free, the "enchanted prince" (as the fish claims to be) grants the wish of the fisherman's wife. That might have been the end of the story, except for an additional detail that the Grimm brothers provide. We are told that the fisherman grows uneasy when reaching the shore, because the once clear sea has become turbid, yellow, and green.

47

In a week or two, the woman demands that her husband go back to the sea, which is now dense, purple, dark blue, and gray. The fisherman entreats the flounder to replace the new house with a palace. The Grimm brothers tell readers how reluctant the man is to proceed. Despite entertaining no grounds for making this request, the husband chooses to try to honor his wife's desire.

Once again, the flounder grants the wish. Living in a stone palace with marble floors and gold tapestries dispels the husband's doubts and reservations. His spouse decides to sleep on the matter, however, because she harbors a nagging doubt that the palace is not quite good enough.

Waking up early, the wife proclaims that she wants to be crowned a king. Lost in her fantastic obsession is the fact that her partner plainly has no interest in being elevated as her consort. No matter: in order to extend the plot, the Grimm brothers reiterate an increasingly familiar sequence of events. The insatiable wife sends her increasingly uneasy and distressed husband back to ask the flounder for a gift, one befitting a palatial lifestyle. Once again the fish accedes. Once again upward mobility, rather than stifling regal delusions, distresses her spouse. Guess what happens next....

Two weeks later, the husband (whom the Grimm brothers clearly portray as more frightened than tired) trudges back to the shoreline, where he encounters a dark, dense, raging sea. *Now* his wife wants to sit upon an imperial throne, he tells the fish. Although an emperor already rules in the realm, the enchanted prince of a flounder nonetheless accedes. The husband returns home to behold his wife wearing a crown three yards high, set with gems.

Ruling over an empire proves not enough, so the wife determines to become pope. This latest request is very wrong, judges the fisherman, but opportunities for marital reasoning have long since passed. Although *he* does not want to annoy the fish, the husband (portrayed in this scene as a very sick man) leaves the castle to return to the sea.

There, he finds the shore shrouded in clouds so low that they touch the roaring, boiling waters. The flounder nonetheless grants this demand, too. When he arrives home, his exultant wife is wearing papal robes and a triple tiara.

Sleepless that night, the wife wakes up with a plea "to become equal to God." OMG, the husband thinks—now she wants dominion over the sun, moon, and heavens! Even so, the compliant fisherman begs the flounder, as the transactions have been effected in the past. This time, finally, the wife has overstepped her bounds. The fish declares, "Just go home; your wife is sitting in the filthy old pigsty again." The sea becomes calm the moment the flounder dismisses the disgraced fisherman.

In both summary and detailed versions of *The Fisherman and His Wife*, the Grimm brothers have crafted a linear plot line. The main characters in their tale operate literally and figuratively on parallel plains. And the fable unfolds with the *dramatis personae* performing invariably at cross purposes.

The peasant acts as if he were a saintly fisher of men. For much of his life the man has gone about his daily routine without much luck. Then, like St. Peter, he encounters an enchanted figure. Note that the flounder and the fisherman meet by the deep sea, situated symbolically between the realms of life and death.

Does the fish represent Christ? (After all, *Ichthys* means "fish" in ancient Greek. It is an acronym translated in English as "Jesus Christ, Son of God, [Our] Savior.") The Son of Man was baptized in water, yet the biblical Messiah is never heralded by a magic incantation. Nor does this mysterious flounder make unconditional promises about the grace of happiness or eternal life. The fish in *The Fisherman and His Wife* basically wishes to save its gills and be set free. Reparations come later, orchestrated by a third character.

That third character in the Grimm's narrative is the wife, who effortlessly exploits her spouse's obligingly compliant ways. The malcontent commands her husband to negotiate a series of transactions, each of which (she adamantly insists) will quench her desire for material entitlements yielding higher status, power, and wealth.

The Grimm brothers' parabolic fable begins as an innocent fairy tale and ends on a sobering, somber note. Few listeners or readers, I suspect, are surprised by the denouement. Who could miss the mounting tension shadowing characters who seem unwilling or unable to heed warning signs?

Perhaps children are at a disadvantage in responding to this query. Kids rarely project their reactions onto adult characters. And youngsters, at least ones who do not read between the lines, leave a host of questions unanswered. Do children grasp the folly of a grown man too eager to please his spouse? Can they empathize with the fisherman's relentless compromises in successive encounters with "the enchanted prince?" Are they old enough to realize that the fisherman increasingly finds his role as an interlocutor to be distasteful, tiring, and sickening? Are young listeners sufficiently aware that big people make mistakes and overstep bounds? Do they realize that their child-like impulse to have their needs satiated parallels the wife's desire for more creature comforts and greater adulation?

Truth be told: how far would any of us—young or old—willfully or sheepishly dare to initiate any transactions with that cold fish? Do we really believe that the flounder is an enchanted prince? How long would it take us to suspect that the flounder may be a trickster, claiming to be an accommodating, generous gift-giver? When do we get the tragic truths that enliven this seemingly comedic fable? When is enough finally enough?

Each of the characters in *The Fisherman and His Wife* makes decisions—or at least is portrayed as needing to make choices. Neither the fisherman, the wife, nor the flounder appears to weigh potential failures against likely successes. They almost never tally up wins over losses in a detached, likely disillusioned, manner. How often, after all, do peasants become kings, emperors, or popes? Does craving dominion over creation entitle us to confer upon ourselves ineffable powers of divinity? No one wants to spend their last days in a pigsty, but do not all of us live into death, eventually crossing the sea?

Elders can use their extra years to derive subtle interpretations of *The Fisherman and His Wife*. Some lessons from this tale will trouble them more acutely than their offspring may realize. Most adults sooner or later accept the fact that humans live in a world beyond their control. Is this not manifest as Nature colors the drama? The sea is calm in the first scene, then becomes darker and more turbulent, only to return in the last act to its pristine state.

Forces of Nature complement dialogues and transactions in the Grimms' fable. First, the fisherman lets his wife's incessant demands overrule his own inner voices of conflict. Nature presents him with clues that he chooses to ignore. Experiencing increasing despair, to which his wife is oblivious, the husband is blind to the possibility that the flounder expresses displeasure.

Second, the fisherman's wife assumes that riches and power are bound to enhance the quality of married life. Has it never occurred to her that material and existential losses might diminish the accretion of good fortune? Does the woman deny the inevitability of death? (The Grimms' fable was not intended to be a religious morality tale, however much its narrative parallels Eve eating the forbidden fruit before she and Adam are tossed out of the Garden.) Pursuing status and opulence—insatiable goals for many in the prime of life—does not guarantee happily successful aging, especially if they are realized in advancing years of frailty.

Third, the tale reflects that misunderstandings cloud adult perspectives. The couple do not communicate effectively; they are portrayed as incapable of understanding one another. And for all we know, the conversations between the fisherman and the flounder may resemble a charade until the pair's last dialogue. By then, it is too late to reverse fortunes. Finally, the flounder, too, is a victim in *The Fisherman and His Wife*. The story, after all, hinges on the fish's resistance to becoming a tasty meal. And, living in a sea that grows darker and darker, surely "the enchanted prince" must have known that it could not satisfy requests forever. Princes may demand deference and privileges, but there is no earthly place for two emperors, popes, or gods.

To me, the story underscores some differences in ways that children and older people perceive the world. The Grimms' childlike message takes on disturbingly fresh meaning when read in later life. Nor were the fabulists alone in contrasting youth and age. The theme appears in *The Sage's* Tao Te Ching: *Ancient Advice for the Second Half of Life*:

The youth is fearless out of foolishness.
The sage is fearless out of wisdom.
The youth feel invulnerable and acts without awareness.
The sage knows vulnerability and acts with mindful care.
The youth has strength but does not know the Tao.
The sage seems weak but accesses the power of All Things....
I see myself for who I am.
No illusions. Great serenity.

Among the great gifts of advancing years is a willingness to accept limits. Weakness and vulnerability, paradoxically, can be sources of wisdom and strength. Tempering outlandish quests for aggrandizement requires more than disillusionment or disinterest, because we have considerable leeway in deciding how to compose our lives. We may hesitate to let go of pride and egotism, but we can choose to do so. "Great serenity," declares the venerable Chinese poet, arises only through facing up to and trying to resolve worldly tensions. Ideally, we can search for authentic meaning in All Things.

CHAPTER 5

Jack and the Beanstalk

BILL

A poor country lad named Jack trades the family cow for a handful of magic beans, which then grow into an enormous beanstalk reaching up into the clouds. Jack climbs the beanstalk and finds himself in the castle of an unfriendly giant who senses Jack's presence and cries, "Fee, fie, fo, fum, I smell the blood of an Englishman!" Outwitting the giant, Jack retrieves an enchanted goose that lays golden eggs and escapes with it down the beanstalk. The giant pursues him but falls to his death when Jack chops the beanstalk out from under him. Jack and his mother go on to live happily—and prosperously—ever after.

*J*ack *be nimble, Jack be quick … Jack Frost, Jack Sprat, Jack and Jill … Hit the road, Jack. Slip out the back, Jack …* Jack certainly gets around! And now—in this best known of the "Jack Tales" of English and American folklore—here he is clambering up a beanstalk, coming up against a giant, and making off with a magical goose that dispenses golden eggs. What am I to make of his odd adventures, now that I'm seventy-plus?

Come to think of it, I'm half Jack myself. My son and I are forever calling each other by the silly nicknames that we dreamed up for one another many years ago. For reasons that are lost to me now, I was christened "BobbyJack." So, then, let me tap into my inner Jack and toy with how this beanstalk business speaks to me since it first burrowed its way into what Francis Spufford enchantingly dubs "the chambers of [my] imagination."

In his delightful volume, *The Child that Books Built*, Spufford tells us how he has "gone back and read again the sequence of books that carried me from babyhood to the age of 19" and "tried to become again the reader I had been when I encountered each for the first time, wanting to know how my particular history, in my particular family, at that particular time, had ended up making me into the reader [and the person] I am today." He concludes with the wistful observation that "the true story of my life ... is just a story among stories, and after I have been reading for a while, I can hardly tell any more what is my own."

Thinking back over the countless tales that have entered the chambers of my own imagination, my question is much the same: Where does my story begin and Jack's story end? What themes in his story are mirrored in mine?

I can't pinpoint how or by whom I was first introduced to this tale. I'm trying to remember, for example, whether my parents ever read to me at all. I clearly recall reading lots to myself. Curled up in my favorite chair in the living room of our house, a stack of thickly-buttered Stoned Wheat Thins as my treat, I inhaled installment after installment of The Hardy Boys series, my all-time favorites. Up until quite recently, in fact, I would pull one of them off my shelves and reread it, to recapture some of the feeling that I'd felt years before in following a story whose plot was comfortingly predictable and whose storyworld refreshingly unambiguous, compared to the complex realities of my own life as a middle-aged adult.

I dabbled too, of course, in Nancy Drew books, not to mention the Trixie Belden series, works that my sisters had lying around. And I remember the Danny Orlis books as well, which were Hardy Boys for Christians, the aim in each volume being not just to figure out whodunit but to lead whodunit to the Lord.

As for fairy tales, with their improbable plots and (on the surface) uncomplicated characters, I was exposed to them so early that I didn't so much read them as ingest them, to the point where they became encoded in my DNA. In the case of Jack, what got encoded is the first of seven basic narrative patterns that are said to run through the world of stories everywhere: pulp fiction, fairy tales, and high literature alike. It is *overcoming the monster*. The one who overcomes—whatever form the monster takes: a demon, an alien, a murderous spouse, a repressive regime, a killer epidemic—is, of course, the hero. And in tales such as these the hero invariably prevails.

To make sure we're on the same page, let me venture a summary of the central storyline—or at least my version thereof, for apparently there are several, reaching back hundreds of years.

Jack lives with his mother (the father is departed or dead, we're not told which) and they're poor, very poor, with a single cow to sustain them. When its milk dries up, mother sends Jack to market to sell it and, with the profit, buy seeds to plant crops that will sustain them longer-term. En route, however, he's stopped by a strange old man who tricks him into exchanging the cow for three magic beans. Thinking this seems not a bad deal, Jack gives the man the cow and, beans in hand, heads back home. Disgusted by Jack's gullibility, his mother tosses them out the window and sends him to bed without his supper. When he wakens next morning, he looks out his window to the sight of an enormous beanstalk reaching up into the clouds. Curious, not to mention famished, and having nothing left to lose, he makes his way skyward, limb by limb, until he emerges into a beautiful, sprawling landscape where, at the end of a winding lane, sits a massive castle. As he approaches it, a woman giant with only one eye catches sight of him (albeit myopically) and invites him inside where, out of pity perhaps, she offers him breakfast. Soon, though, Jack hears the thunderous thump-thump of her even more gigantic husband, whom she informs Jack loves nothing better for his own breakfast than little boys broiled on toast. *Fee-fi-fo-fum*, the giant roars, *I smell the blood of an Englishman* ...

From here on, versions vary widely, and debates therefore rage over specific elements: Did the golden harp that played by itself have the face of a young woman, and was winning her favor part of Jack's motivation to steal her (or it) away? Was it a goose that laid the golden eggs or merely a hen? Did Jack climb the beanstalk three times or only once? Did ...? And so on and so forth. But apart from these factual-textual matters, which are best left to experts in folklore to adjudicate, there's the matter of how the tale as a whole is to be taken. The two most dominant interpretations, it seems, have been a Freudian one and a Marxist one.

The Freudian perspective is captured in Bruno Bettleheim's classic book *The Uses of Enchantment: The Meaning and Importance of Fairy Tales*, where he employs sweeping statements like "climbing up the beanstalk symbolizes the 'magic' power of the phallus to rise, but also a boy's feelings connected with masturbation." And, not surprisingly, Jack's tussle with the giant is seen as Oedipal in essence. The merits of such a reading I don't totally dispute, of course, particularly the Oedipal bit, though, honestly, I find it overdrawn.

As for a Marxist reading, the tale is an allegory in which Jack and his mother stand for the downtrodden of the planet. Mr and Mrs Giant, on the other hand, symbolize the evils of the capitalist system and the one percent of the world's population who get richer and richer at the expense of the other ninety-nine. Meanwhile, Jack cutting down the beanstalk and thus slaying the giant amounts to the triumph of the proletariat and the ushering in of a golden age of justice for all. Again, a good enough interpretation but equally overdrawn, and ultimately unhelpful in shedding light on my own life in particular.

Naturally, there are many elements I could zero in on: the golden harp, the golden eggs, the beanstalk itself, to say nothing of the giant's wife or Jack's mother or the old man who conned him into exchanging the cow for the beans—more elements than I can attend to properly here. So, if I may, I'll focus on the giant.

While I was sharing with her my musings on the meaning of the story, my (then) partner took me by surprise when she began championing the giant's side. As far as she was concerned, he and his wife were simply minding their own business, hanging out in their castle, doing what giants do, when out of nowhere, this young upstart trespasses onto their property, robs them of their main source of income (the goose) and of pleasure (the harp), skedaddles back to earth, and promptly chops down the beanstalk, causing the poor, bumbling giant, who clambers down after him in justifiable pursuit, to tumble to his death. I found myself thinking, "She has a point."

Surely, giants are not by definition bad. They're not automatically ogres or Goliaths just because they're big. They can't help their size, their height, their body type. It's who they are. In fact, because they soar above the crowd, the poor things probably get teased a lot, bullied, other-ed. My son, for example, who's been markedly taller and wider than me ever since he was a teen, is as kind as they come. A gentle giant, I think of him—*The Friendly Giant*—the title of a TV show that ran from the late 1950s to the mid-1980s and was a boon companion for many a Canadian kid.

I remember attending a church service one Thanksgiving Sunday back in my seminary days. As part of a congregational prayer, the worship leader invited us to stand up wherever we were sitting and voice aloud one thing for which we were especially grateful. I recall this one white-haired gentleman, stooped of stature, possibly a retired academic, rising slowly to his feet and humbly announcing, "I give thanks for the giants on whose shoulders I've been privileged to stand."

My giants include all the teachers, thinkers, and authors, and all the narrative scholars for sure, whose ideas have enabled me to see much further than I could have ever seen by myself; to think thoughts, feel feelings, and formulate perspectives (on aging, for instance) that I couldn't have formulated on my own. I'm not discounting my intelligence, simply acknowledging the legacy of research and experience—the centuries-rich heritage of ideas and definitions, distinctions and discoveries, even dead ends—that I have drawn upon continually in my years in higher education and, I dare to hope, have helped to extend a modest measure more.

Giants can be bad, but giants can be good. They can be malignant or benign, foul or fair. And they can be both at once. This leads me once more to thoughts of my father, who was surely a gigantic figure in my life, and, all things considered, a positive one as well. I can't stress this enough. He was, all in all, a good man, a good minister, and a good dad. Alongside many of my male friends, the "daddy issues" with which I've had to deal—as men have done in all eras, in all cultures, everywhere—are comparatively innocuous. Still, they're there all the same, and they need to be noted. For Dad, as I say, had a dark, mercurial side, and even (to my mind) a monstrous side. It was a side he couldn't help perhaps, a side rooted in frustrations with married life or family life (where he was the proverbial king of the castle), or in his God-given personality, or in unresolved issues with his own father in turn, in line with the scriptural adage about "the sins of the father." Whatever the reasons, it was a side that, as a kid, I hated and feared. Here's the sort of scenario I have in mind.

"Go down in the basement and get me that Robertson screwdriver with the blue handle," he'd bark at me impatiently, impatient less with me, I've since accepted, than with himself, because of his ineptness at carpentry or home repair or whatever task it was that we'd be working on. "It's hanging on the rack above the workbench." I'd scamper down to the basement as quickly as I could, sensing his fuse burning lower by the minute. I'd stand in front of the workbench and look from one end of it to the other at the tools that were hanging on the pegboard above it. But I scanned my environment in vain. In fact, I wasn't quite sure what a Robertson screwdriver even was. Yet, the anxiety tightening in my chest, there was no way I was going back to him and ask.

In similar situations since, such as scanning the shelves of my office for a particular book, rather than look for it systematically from left to right, my eyes will dart back and forth and up and down until, more often than not, I fail to find it at all. It might only be the following day, without even trying, that I finally lay eyes on it. It's basically a problem with my vision, some form of dyslexia or attention deficit disorder, I don't know what, but not a problem with my intelligence per se. In any case, I'd finally have to go back outside to where my father was fuming over the challenge at hand. But my own hand would be empty. "I couldn't find it, Dad," I'd confess to him, shaking in my boots. "What do you mean, you couldn't find it?!" he'd snort back. "I told you! It's there above the workbench, right where I put it." "I'm really sorry, Dad, but I just can't find it." "GO BACK DOWN AND LOOK!" he'd storm, his ire rising by the second.

More frazzled than ever, I'd return to the basement and repeat the procedure, again to no avail. The scene that awaited me was certain to be scary. When I came back again empty-handed, or worse still, with another screwdriver that I knew wasn't the right one but might possibly do the trick, he'd cuff me across the head and yell "Jee-suz, don't be so STUPID. I'll have to go down there myself!" Ready to pee my pants from fear and self-loathing, I'd be shown, sure enough, where the screwdriver was hanging, exactly like he'd said. "Now what did I tell you?!" he'd demand, convinced no doubt that this was a teachable moment in my formation as a reliable employee and that it was his fatherly duty to drive home the point, no matter the cost. "You told me to pay attention," I'd sheepishly reply. "Yes. PAY ATTENTION," he retorted, "and do as you're told!"

It wasn't always like this, of course. There were certain things we did together that bordered on fun, or at least weren't entirely unenjoyable, things that permitted us a measure of father-son ca-maraderie: things like building a slot-car racetrack in the basement out of plywood and papier-mâché, or like digging tunnels in the snow. Things that, at the very least, afforded me some relief. Like taking a trailer full of garbage to the dump, because by the time we did a dump run it was usually the end of the day and all possible occasions to get told I was stupid were largely behind us. Still, I've carried this sense of being stupid through more of my life than I'm comfortable admitting: a nagging self-doubt about my cleverness, about the merits of my writing, the effectiveness of my teaching— you name it. Not just stupid in the sense of others' opinion of me, but stupid in the sense of some essential quality that, at bottom, I embody. I carried this feeling to Harvard, in fact, which, paradox-ically, did little to alleviate it. It made it worse almost, surrounded as I was every day by the best and the brightest, the loudest and vainest, from the largest, most prestigious prep schools in the land. Harvard, too, was a giant in my life, one that lured lads like me to its lair from far and wide, only to chew us up and spit us out four years later as "educated men," primed to scoot up every beanstalk we could find.

Meanwhile back at Dad … in due course, I found my ways to cut him down to size in my own psyche, which is where it most counts. Not all at once, admittedly. Not in one fell chop, but gradually, incrementally, with a chip here and a chip there—a chip off the old block. And not, for the most part, intentionally either, although to my credit, in my mid-twenties, I once told him to "f… off"—something that a few of my friends confided in me that they'd have told him long before if he'd been *their* father instead! But if there was one main turning-point in our relationship, one that signaled my beginning to come out from under his influence over my life, it would be when, at the age of thirty-seven, having been at it for a decade, I decided it was time to exit parish ministry—a vocation that I had followed him into without, as I look back now, thinking things through thoroughly for myself. But after a series of experiences that I can only describe as synchronistic, I experienced this overwhelming push to return to university, to tap into a swirl of curiosities that had been set in motion during my seminary days, and to work toward my doctorate, though toward what kind of career it might take me I wasn't quite clear.

Some thirteen years earlier, I'd undertaken a similar challenge at Cambridge—yet another giant in my life—when I enrolled to do a Ph.D.. I bailed out nine months later, however, because in terms of my chosen topic (autobiography and religion), I had bitten off far more than I could possibly chew, to say nothing of lacking the needed self-discipline to finish my dissertation in anything approaching a timely or affordable fashion. It was an experience of failure that I continue to be plagued by and have dreams about—feverish, convoluted reveries about returning to England at my present age and, by hook or by crook, completing my degree.

In retrospect, my decision to leave the ministry was the best I could have made, and in some ways it made me! It meant breaking free of a line of work that was intriguing and fulfilling, to be sure, but overwhelming as well, that was stealing "me" away from me. Most importantly, it meant breaking free of my father's aspirations for me, a man who had fantasized openly at one point, for instance, about the two of us going on the road together as a father-son evangelistic team, preaching our way across the land and rescuing souls for the

Lord. It meant setting out on my own road instead, on the "hero's journey," as Joseph Campbell would say, throwing caution to the wind and following my "bliss" wherever it would lead.

That journey—which I like to think is far from finished—turned out to be far from straightforward. Following completion of my dissertation, it took me a further eight years of wandering in the wilderness from one short-term contract to another before finally, at fifty, I squeaked my way onto the tenure track and began crawling up the academic ladder—the beanstalk par excellence for those whose lives are built by books.

The higher I climbed—*every rung goes higher, higher*—the more Dad admired me. The deep approval, the unconditional acceptance, which I'd craved from him for much of my life—each time I embarked on some new venture, or bought a new car, or brought home a new publication or partner—began coming far more frequently and sincerely than ever before. That said, it came somewhat grudgingly at first. At base, he was befuddled as to why I would abandon a perfectly promising career as a preacher, making my way safely up the ecclesiastical ladder toward ever more prestigious congregations, and instead take a leap of faith into the uncertain, underpaid world of academe. My suspicion, in fact, is that he was secretly satisfied when I aborted my Cambridge adventure and skulked back to Canada to set out at last on the more useful and, to him, more familiar adventure of parish ministry. For, however bright he was, he had an anti-intellectual streak. His go-to reading was hardly the Harvard Classics, let alone the Bible, and certainly not any of my own books, but those of Louis L'Amour, which are basically Hardy Boys for men. When I was inclined to fits of hyper-pensivity in college, he would quote Shakespeare at me: "Cassius has a lean and hungry look; / he thinks too much." Then, after earning my second master's degree in theology, he jauntily offered the opinion that, if I were lucky enough, I might just be able to cash in my various diplomas, toss in an extra fifty cents, and get myself a cup of coffee.

Gradually, though, his admiration grew, until by my early sixties I was certain of it. It was palpable almost, as if he could see at last that my somewhat dreamy, distracted nature—so bad for finding screwdrivers but so good for writing books—was paying off in a way that he could measure. Each spring he was genuinely keen to browse through the annual report that my university required me to compile, listing off the courses I'd taught, students I'd su-pervised, grants I'd received, presentations I'd made, and articles I'd published. His eagerness was additionally intense, of course, because my successes were due largely to the blend of interests in both aging and stories that the two of us shared—intellectually, for me, and instinctively, for him. Finally, we had found ourselves some common ground. It was Narrative Gerontology, which, ca-reer-wise, has very much been the goose that lays the golden eggs, my ticket to travel further in this world than I could ever have imagined, not just culturally and scholastically but personally, even spiritually, too. He would cart around a copy of my CV in the seat of his walker as he shuffled down the hallway to the lobby of the senior-friendly apartment complex where he and mother lived until their nineties, happy to brag me up to the other men he'd pass the afternoons with: "This is my son, the narrative gerontologist, in whom I am well pleased."

Yes, at long last, I cut him down to size. But it wasn't just me. It was the ravages of age itself, particularly the arthritis, which made getting around at all an exercise in agony, which oddly enough tem-pered his temper, and which reduced him to humble desperation for the least measure of relief—like the kind he received from me, for instance, from the back rubs, the hip rubs, and the bum rubs that I gave him, more or less willingly, every other day towards the end. "Thank you, sooo much, Bill," he would say to me, sweetly and sincerely, his bedroom reeking of Voltaren or Icy Hot or whatever other product promised reprieve from his pain.

Happily, he lived long enough, and so did I, for the two of us to work out most of our issues in an unspoken, organic manner. As far as the story of our relationship is concerned, Shakespeare would likely agree: "all's well that ends well." Indeed, I was with him in the Emergency Room the night that he died, an odd yet tender experience that I'm forever grateful to have had. Unlike tons of other men I've known, our relationship was blessed with sufficient time to ripen to where we were no longer Giant and Jack but father and son, in the mellowest way that fathers and sons can taste.

To be sure, there have been other giants in my life, good and bad, and these reflections have set my mind spinning about their impact upon me as well. But let me rein in my thoughts here a little by singling out one giant in particular that, in my heart, is linked to Dad, one that you might say is the elephant in the room as far as many of the themes are concerned that we're looking into in this book. I'm talking about … The Mysterium Tremendum, The Alpha and Omega, The Creator, The Divine, "that than which," as Anselm says, "nothing greater can be conceived." I mean the Cosmic He, She, or It, The Source or The Force or whatever you care to call it—God, Our Father, or, in William Blake's impious phrase, Nobodaddy.

Like many who started out in a conventional religious community, in my case a community over which Dad, as minister, presided, my imagination conceived of this giant as up there, above the clouds: a grand old man seated upon a throne, with a long white beard and a kindly but inscrutable nature, whose thoughts are not our thoughts and whose ways are not our ways. As a kid, I felt that Dad's ways and God's ways were in fact not that far apart, the mercurial might of Jehovah's ways in particular: the God of the Old Testament, high and lifted up, more than that of the New, the Incarnate One, the Word made Flesh and dwelling among us.

With time, however, and with the natural maturing of my imagination—and thanks to my reading of all sorts of books that highlight the fine line between physics and metaphysics, between science and spirituality—my relationship with this giant at the end (or heart) of the universe has changed a great deal as well. My concept of "God" has also been cut down to size, Transcendence being balanced by Immanence, by a "sense sublime / of something far more deeply interfused," in Wordsworth's words; a presence "closer to us than breathing and nearer than hands and feet," as Tennyson would say, in whom—not *under* whom but *in* whom—we live and move and have our being. This kind of radical immanence, this consummate down-to-earth-ness, I find articulated powerfully by a thinker for whom science and spirituality were effectively fused: Pierre Teilhard de Chardin. Here's a glimpse into his vision of reality from his haunting little book, *Hymn of the Universe*:

> Every force which moves through me, envelops me, or captivates me emanates from the divine will as its fundamental source ... Thus every contact, whether it caresses me, pierces me, bruises me, jostles me ... or crushes me, is a contact with one of the forms, multiple but in every case adorable, of the hand of God. God, too, is the source of all the elements of which I am composed. ... God is vibrant in the ether and through it he penetrates to the very marrow of my material being. By the ether all material bodies are joined, influence one another, and support one another in the unity of the vast sphere whose ultimate boundary we cannot even imagine.

As a baby boomer, I'm one of that generation of men who have been drawn to the writings of Robert Bly. Granted, I haven't (yet) gone the route of beating drums around the campfire at weekend retreats in the forest, venting my tensions around being a man or a son, tuning into my inner Iron John, and generally feeling what one thinker calls "fire in the belly." But I've been a member of a few men's groups in the past thirty-odd years, and am part of one at present. Ranging in age from sixty-five to eighty-five, six of us gather once a month to focus on our experience of The Spirit, employing a combination of Quaker meditation and respectful, soulful conversation to probe an assortment of issues in our lives and our relationships, and to deepen our spiritual development overall. We call ourselves the "Wise Space" and there's not much that would keep me from missing our meetings. The fellowship (literally) that we share for these two hours every month has enriched me immensely, heightening my sense sublime of a Something or a Someone that is deeply interfused with the fabric of my life.

By the end of our little tale, Jack has completed his hero's journey and, through wiliness and gutsiness, transformed himself from a naïve lad duped into trading the family cow for a handful of beans to a young man capable of facing his fears, slaying a giant, and saving the day. Aspects of my own journey, which I hope holds still more adventures up ahead, are mirrored amusingly, I find, in Jack's journey, too. As far as my tussles with giants are concerned, I can hardly tell any more where his story ends and my own story starts.

CHAPTER 6

The Rich Young Ruler

BARBARA

A certain young ruler asked Jesus, "Good Teacher, what must I do to inherit eternal life?" Jesus said to him, "Why do you call me good? No one is good but God alone. You know the commandments: 'You shall not commit adultery; You shall not murder; You shall not steal; You shall not bear false witness; Honor your father and mother.'" The ruler replied, "I have kept all these since my youth." When Jesus heard this, he said to him, "There is still one thing lacking. Sell all that you own and distribute the money to the poor, and you will have treasure in heaven; then come, follow me." But when the man heard this, he became sad; for he was very rich. Jesus looked at him and said, "How hard it is for those who have wealth to enter the kingdom of God!"

In some ways, this is a rather sad story about a good, solid, caring man who has thus far lived a responsible, upright life, having done all that was required of him. Seeking the proffered reward of eternal life, he asks what other requirements, if any, there might be.

There is no suggestion in the story of a self-satisfied smugness, or an assumption that eternal life is guaranteed to him. But when he hears the—frankly, outrageous and totally irresponsible—requirement, he goes away, despairing.

One of the admirable qualities of the way he has lived his life has been his responsibility: he has safeguarded his wealth, not squandered it. He could have gone to a casino and lost all his money without breaking any of those commandments. Instead, he has not only obeyed all the commandments but also been prudent enough that he still has quite a bit of wealth. Is he now to be punished for his conscientiousness?

Is Jesus suggesting that the man should have wasted or thrown away the money, been irresponsible? He then wouldn't be so burdened by his wealth that he would be denied permission to enter the Kingdom, but he also would have nothing left to give to the poor in the future. If we have anything of worth, are we to just get rid of it? The demand Jesus makes seems senseless. It might have been reasonable if he had said, "Go to a good actuary, estimate what you'll need to support yourself until you die, and give the rest to the charities of your choice." For that matter, he might simply have suggested that the man continue to live, maybe a bit more sparingly, and make sure to leave a will giving his entire estate to the poor. But no, the demand is that he get rid of it all, now. Are we to be irresponsible with what we have, so that we are poor enough to enter the Kingdom? Refuse to use our money, our privilege, while we have them, even to benefit those less fortunate? Jesus' demand really seems based less on how to benefit others, and more on how to deprive ourselves.

In fact, I suspect that it is the seduction—of money, of power, of position, of fame, of beauty—that Jesus is attempting to stem. When we have such riches, we can come to rely on the assurances they give us: perhaps the assurance of superiority, but especially that of control. We can live as if we are in charge. Despite the knowledge that we all die, we can try to convince ourselves that, with our excellent medical care, we can stave off death (or at least control its timing, the severity of illness, the type of physical limitations, and the degree of pain) by buying our way into healthcare services that will negate the power of our decline. Our money, power, and prestige can, in fact, provide a buffer between us and much of the world's pain. And we may, as a result, come to rely on that protective power and begin to think that we are in charge not just of our present life, but of our future, as well.

But the man's question is about eternal life; why is he concerned about dying at this point? There is no indication that he has had any intimations of impending death, so why now? Is it possible that he feels some lack in his *current* life? Is he afraid that he doesn't deserve his power and riches, and that they will be taken away? Or does he see in Jesus' followers something he wants but doesn't have? What might that be? A sense of fellowship and mutual caring? An inner satisfaction clearly *not* rooted in power or material goods? Some serenity or certitude he lacks? Maybe he envies their belief that they are at peace, and that the source of that contentment *cannot* be taken away, because it doesn't depend on transient material goods.

Maybe the young man has an uncomfortable sense that he has been cosseted throughout his life—protected from the cruelties and pains that afflict those without wealth and power. Perhaps he is aware that he is getting older, and it has occurred to him that his riches have always kept him safe from dangers faced by the people over whom he rules. Will his wealth follow him into the afterlife and protect him there? Or will his death be total, and he will be annihilated? For that matter, what if he loses it all *now*?

Possibly the ruler is looking ahead, and becoming afraid of physical debility, an aspect of life that his wealth cannot control. Or maybe it is simply that all the consolations of wealth are not sufficient to ward off a general anxiety and malaise. Many people, perhaps particularly those who have led lucky, privileged lives, or those who have overcome adversity to achieve "the good life," may experience some disillusionment. Is that all there is? Why don't I feel fully satisfied? We may feel that "the good life" isn't all that we assumed it would be—or should be. What is missing?

As we age, we may feel that youth and health are what are missing. If we only had what we have, including the wisdom we've acquired, and also had the youth and health to fully engage in all that the world has to offer, we might be able to truly enjoy life—which may be another way of suggesting that we'd like a certain *kind* of eternal life, one with mature wisdom and no physical or material challenges. Maybe this is the rich ruler's problem. He is troubled enough to approach an itinerant preacher who has no money and a ragtag band of followers to ask him how he can have eternal life.

I wonder whether he and Jesus are even speaking the same language. Jesus answers his question by talking of "the kingdom of God." Is the young ruler open to living in a different realm—this "kingdom of God"—or is he really just wondering about how he might be guaranteed that his current situation will never end? It seems as if the two may be very different propositions. As we see his sadness when asked to give up all his things, we can well imagine his disappointment and puzzlement. The man's efforts have been recognized by the Good Teacher; he has indeed done all that has been required of him. Now what he needs is to give up all the things with which his obedience (and, of course, his luck of being born into privilege) have provided him. He is asked to give up all he has in order to get... what?

The rich young ruler seems to think he is being offered a life—his current life, but devoid of all wealth—that will go on forever. The trade-off isn't worth it to him, and he leaves, to return to his life of money and power—and death. We are given the sense that the author felt the choice is a poor one—that what Jesus offers is more valuable than what the man has chosen. What might Jesus' version of eternal life be? What would be worth giving up all the material goods he has and the life of comfort they provide? What would be worth giving up an accepted belief in his wealth- and power-given superiority over the less fortunate? Shedding his power, his position? No mention is made of any relationships he has—maybe there is none as important for him as his wealth; or perhaps none that would last in the face of poverty.

There are those today who promise a kind of eternal life—for example, cryogenic life, in which the body is frozen until that future day when human life is eternalized and the forces of death and decay have been mastered at last. The frozen corpse will hopefully be able to be resurrected, and those living at that future time will not be subject to physical disease. The financial price may be high, but there is provision for the buyer to set aside what they hope will be significant funds for future life. (Let's leave aside the sheer numbers of potential humans, and the effect of that on the limited resources of the planet; let us posit a livable universe of endless planetary resources to match our endless lives.)

The concept of endless life has had many imaginative expressions. In *Gulliver's Travels*, for instance, Jonathan Swift describes people called Struldbrugs who age but do not die, and increasingly experience their endless lives as dreadfully tedious. The repetitiveness and lack of novelty, even in challenges, is draining. This bleak rendering might, of course, be reimagined to emphasize the endless fascinating surprises and challenges that life can provide. Nonetheless, eternal life, in the sense of an endless extension of our current existence, would appear to have some serious limitations of joy, even in the presence of great wealth.

It may, then, be that we wouldn't actually want endless physical life. It may be that we really just don't want to face the possibility that it could end *right now*, or in a week, or at some other unknown time. As we age, what we want may precisely be the assurance that we are in control: that we are not subject to the loss of loved ones, to the pain and humiliation of illness, to untimely (or even timely) death. To the degree that our money and privilege have protected us from life's most difficult horrors and tribulations, we may rely on what assurance they offer as we come ever closer to the diminutions we increasingly face. But sooner or later we are forced to accept that the power of money, fame, professional reputation, good health, powerful friends, and so forth, is fleeting. All such powers are lovely to have, and they may cushion us from a great deal of pain. But they do not stave off, among other ills, family discord, abandonment, natural disasters, accidental death or destruction, much less death as a natural end to life. Despite our best efforts, we are not able to prevent searing pain and loss in our lives. We have little or no control over many of the aspects of life, including death, which cause the most anxiety and fear.

And yet, we often see in people—young or old—who are nearing death a peace that seems not rational. There are, of course, those who, until the last, display an anger or fear that is wholly understandable, but many people at the brink of death seem to be in a state of exquisite peace. Perhaps that peace is a recognition that leaving everything of this world—wealth, power, even one's loved ones (and one's mind)—is overshadowed by whatever is coming; and that the coming reality is already giving consolation and a willingness to let everything go for the sake of it. Oftentimes, people who have been close to death and then recover find that that sense of consolation remains with them, even if they have no intellectual grasp of what has changed within them. If that "peace which passes understanding" embodies a true sense of death as something to be welcomed rather than feared, how might that inform us *before* we get to the shores of the Rubicon? Might we hold less tightly to what we will have to lose anyway? Or will we choose to cling even more firmly to what we fear losing? Maybe a reliance on money, power, position, and other "worldly" protections—even health—are not, as we often feel them to be, bulwarks of safety, but impediments to seeing the truth more clearly. We are buttressed in our desperate need to believe that we are in charge, because we fear that the alternative—the truth—is too terrifying. Perhaps Jesus was suggesting that facing the realities we fear might be a necessary path to peace.

Jesus may have been suggesting that the young ruler rid himself of his material goods precisely because their loss would mean the loss of his contentment. If he could be content with "nothing left to lose," he would be truly at peace. If we are afraid of losing something—if our contentment requires that we *have* something: wealth, power, health, even a relationship, or our mind—then we will have inevitable anxiety about losing whatever it is we depend on. The story may ask us to examine what we can't live without, and then to see if we might be able to hold it less tightly in order to live in deeper serenity.

It may be, then, that Jesus is speaking of a realm of existence which is extant even now, while we are in this life. We will perhaps each of us conceptualize "eternal life," or "the kingdom of God," in our own way. It seems to me that the story suggests that reliance on things of this world—which we know are neither eternal nor even reliable—is ultimately futile. Nothing material is going to be able to "manage" life and death, loss and pain. It is through relinquishing belief in the power of material things, which are in fact powerless, that we have an opportunity to come to terms with our human powerlessness in general. It may be that we believe in some other power that is in charge of the universe—and us. Maybe we call it God, or Yahweh, or Allah, or Brahma, or Nature. It seems likely that Jesus was pointing to a belief in God which can grant us peace—the peace of believing in something called "eternal life," which may be something like a perfect joining with the eternal source of light and life. Other religions have different conceptualizations of an all-powerful Being, but how many would assert that material possessions, or worldly power, play any role in a life beyond mortality?

And what if there is no other being or force that we can trust to control our lives or the universe beneficently? What of all those who believe either that there is no all-powerful, loving entity or that we cannot know whether or not there is something? Many go a step further into embracing our powerlessness, suggesting that it is nonetheless possible, even in the face of the absolute unknown, to feel reassured that we are *not* in charge. That we can (and perforce must) let go and face the radical unknown. Maybe facing our limitations honestly, accepting the enormity of the realm of life over which we have absolutely no control, may itself—paradoxically—be sufficient to free us from existential angst.

CHAPTER 7

The Ugly Duckling

ANDY

Out from his mother's womb came a bird that did not much resemble a duck—its beak was too long and feathers too scruffy. The ugly duckling, which neither quacked nor swam like the rest of its siblings, ran away. It failed to nest with goslings and had to leave a farm couple's home when it grew large. It finally reached a crystal clear pond in the dead of winter, where the most beautiful specimens he had ever seen were gracefully gliding. There, the protagonist found his niche. The ugly duckling, it turns out, was really a swan with beautiful white feathers.

Alas, I have long identified with this folk tale by Hans Christian Andersen. I was first in the birth order of my family of origin, but I have spent much of my life thinking that I was an "ugly" (which is worse than being a "homely") duckling. Suffice it to say, I have fixated on a disturbing truth that does not resolve itself in what the fabulist intended to be a satisfying and happy ending: All the creatures in the barnyard—not just the other new-born ducklings—judged the mother's lastborn odd. The bird did not look, quack, or swim like the others. The ugly duckling writhed in shame, not really aware of why his "differentness" was so disconcerting, if not downright repulsive. I know what it is to be an odd duck.

Leaving the pond where he was born, the protagonist is subject to further approbation. After waddling through sticks and dung, the muddy, ugly duckling is greeted with suspicion when he joins a flock of geese playing in another pond. Things do not go swimmingly, despite the invitation to belong to a new family. The geese fly away when a hunter and his hound approach. The duckling keeps still and silent. The tack works, ironically, because the hound deems this so-called gosling not worth killing.

The next life transition simply leaves the fable's protagonist feeling rejected, sadder, and weaker. After getting dirtier from wandering through more mud, the duckling approaches a small home where he takes refuge. Why do the householders welcome him to stay? Do the farmer and his wife view him as a future feast? Do they expect him to find a mate and produce more ducklings, for them to devour later on? Instead, he grows bigger, recounts the fabulist, making him harder to maintain. When the couple have no more room in their home, they shoo him out. Shutting the door on a consolatory note, they urge him to keep searching for a family that will offer him love and support.

How desperate would I be if thrust into the duckling's dilemma? How many times could I endure being viewed as odd by kin and by groups of strangers? How long could I deny that my fears of being rejected would come true? What choice did I have but to adapt, somehow, to suffer living in my own skin? No wonder the terrifyingly disillusioned story line chilled me as much as it did the protagonist.

Yet the story concludes on an upbeat note, for all is not lost. When another set of birds admire (and possibly envy) his luminously white feathers, the ugly duckling perceives his true identity: he is a beautiful swan. He spends the rest of his days swimming with birds of his feather. That the farmer and his wife and their newborn greet and feed him embellishes an already happy ending.

Why do I now, long past childhood, identify remnants of my life history with the ugly duckling? Despite my mother's assurances, I still see an uncomely face in the mirror. My well-practiced, self-deprecating humor does not assuage feeling inconspicuous at home, invisible in the company of others. Despite accomplishments later in life, I still manage to wallow in self-pity, especially when I recall adolescent horrors.

I did not wish to stand out; I just wanted to fit in. I remember shame on the baseball field when the coach designated me to be that muddy cushion trampled by athletic hitters rounding third base. Looks mattered as much as embodying a certain style in U.S. suburbia during the 1950s. Alas, I rarely made the A-list: I never got invited to overnight co-ed sleepers; I winced when jocks boasted about their sexual exploits in the locker room. And I cringe when I remember asking my father to drive me and a date (the fourth I asked) to the senior prom. (I was a year younger than my friends, not old enough to get a license. And I only passed the driving test on the third try—hardly a success story.)

Through trial and error, I nonetheless morphed into a liminal figure as a young adult. Knowing that I was never going to fulfill grandiose dreams—and surely not the delusional expectations of my parents, teachers, and friends—I derived a little comfort in taking refuge in doorways. Convinced that I was unworthy of acceptance in close relationships, I constantly competed with myself, peers, and anyone else lurking in the shadows. On the one hand, I kept silent when I felt objectified, frozen when I sensed imminent ambushes, just as the ugly duckling did when the geese flew away from the hunters. On the other hand, I never became the swan I secretly wanted to be, which is just as well since nowadays I ruffle fewer feathers than I did in my prime. I am reasonably comfortable in my own sagging skin.

Perhaps revisiting this fable towards the end of life, as I review the norms and challenges of being human, I face the mirror looking like both an ugly duckling and a swan. That I spent years trying to satisfy egotistical dreams and suppressing nightmares makes me no different from many other birds. Every quest for individuation bumps along, more transitory than transformative.

Towards the end of the day I periodically remind myself of my connection to the humus along the ponds' shores: I was created in dust and I shall return to dust. Yet fears of anguish and pain in an undignified death do not trump the joys I have had in being created as a person, with unique gifts and discernible flaws. I am like birds of a feather, who have been called to experience and share love.

The differences between consignment as an ugly duckling and recognition as a beautiful swan, at the end of the day, matter less than their provisional and circumstantial symbolic meaning. I paraphrase Socrates instead of mouthing Hans Christian Andersen: life is good when I live it for myself, better when I live it for others. And I take to heart the ancient Greek philosopher's moral—I celebrate the meanings of life redolent with unexpectedly grace-filled joys amidst spiritual pain.

CHAPTER 8

The Poor Farmer

BILL

A farmer and his son work their humble plot of land with the aid of their horse. When the horse runs off, the neighbors drop round to express their sympathies. "What a terrible thing!" they say, hoping to console him. Unperturbed, the farmer replies, "Maybe yes, maybe no." Eventually the horse returns, followed by a herd of wild horses. This time the neighbors exclaim, "What a wonderful thing!" "Maybe yes, maybe no," is the farmer's response. While trying to tame one of the wild ones, the son breaks his leg. "How awful!" say the neighbors. "Maybe yes, maybe no," the farmer answers back. When a foreign army invades the region, all the young men for miles around are drafted to do battle, but because of his leg, the son is passed over. "How fortunate for you!" say the neighbors, excited. Once more, "Maybe yes, maybe no," comes the man's reply.

Let me be reckless and state straightaway that, whatever else this ancient Taoist tale might be about, it's about wisdom.

From time to time, we all tend to wonder whether we're getting any wiser as we age, if we're learning anything of genuine importance about ourselves, about Life. Put another way, have we truly *grown* older or merely gotten older? Have we become more evolved or mature than when we were eighteen or forty, or are we just ... different?

Theories of psychological development, like Erik Erikson's for instance, maintain that life pushes us through a set of predictable stages. Not that any one stage is better than those before it, it's just different, and it presents us with a different set of developmental tasks. The task we're presented with in the final stage of Erikson's model is to choose between *ego integrity* and *despair*. To successfully navigate this "crisis," as he calls it, we must submit (consciously or otherwise) to a process of *life review*: of examining and evaluating the story of our life to date. If we do, then the prize we stand to gain, he says, is wisdom. One of few psychologists to discuss wisdom at all, he describes it as "detached concern with life itself, in the face of death itself." While he had more to say on the topic, it's this element of detachment that I'll come back to in a bit.

As luck would have it, wisdom has become a topic of interest to me personally, given that I taught a course on it from time to time at university and, fool that I am, published a book on it with my colleague, Gary Kenyon. And I have kept returning to it in other publications too. That said, I can hardly claim to possess any inside understanding of it, for it's one of those vast, enticing terms—like Life or Love or Time—that resists pinning down. At the same time, it's a quality or capacity or attitude, or whatever it is, that's traditionally been assumed to come with age. Which is hugely ironic, however, insofar as gerontologists have paid it only passing attention—not so much (in fairness) because it's judged unimportant, but because it's too amorphous, too motherhood-and-apple-pie, to handily define, which in turn makes it difficult to measure. And in gerontology, the sole discipline officially focused on aging and its associated issues, if something can't ultimately be measured, it receives short shrift.

Happily, in a few corners of the field, where the focus rises above such practical matters as fall prevention, caregiver burden, Type II diabetes, and cellular aging in mice, researchers have confirmed the emergence of certain modes of thinking in later life that were less natural for us at earlier stages in our development. These include *dualistic thinking*, which means an openness to paradox and contradiction and the general Yin and Yang of things; *relativistic thinking*, which means an acknowledgment of the contingency of all our knowledge, including our knowledge of ourselves; and *systematic thinking*, which means the ability to see the forest—the bigger picture, if you like—and not be unduly distracted by the trees. Leaving such distinctions in the background, let me return, then, to our little story, which hints that wisdom comprises several things at once.

Once when I was a minister in a city church, there was this one particularly open-minded, well-read older woman who exuded an air of being forever on the edge of some astounding insight. One of few women her age in the congregation to hold a university degree, she was co-owner with her husband of a local insurance company. For some reason, she found me moderately intelligent and sought me out for conversation whenever she had the chance. One day, she invited me to join her and her husband for lunch. No sooner had we begun to eat, however, than she burst forth with her latest revelation. What she wanted more than anything else at this stage in her life, she announced with great conviction, was not more knowledge, nor more money, nor more anything except—in the phrase she carefully enunciated—"imperturbable equanimity."

Imperturbable equanimity: hardly a phrase, even in Chinese, that's apt to be uppermost in the vocabulary of the poor farmer in this parable. And yet he remains amazingly calm amid each new situation—horse gone, horse returned, etc.—and to the frustration, no doubt, of his well-intentioned neighbors, he refuses to leap to conclusions. It's not that he's jaded or a cynic. He's circumspect, cautious. It's as if he has taken straight to heart all the sayings we've had trotted out to us since childhood: *Take life as it comes ... Be careful what you wish for ... One day at a time ... This too shall pass.*

"There is nothing either good or bad," Shakespeare assures us in *Hamlet*, "but thinking makes it so." If we accept the poor farmer as our guru on the matter, wisdom entails an element of detachment from the immediacy of circumstances—not coldly or uncaringly so, yet always somewhat disengaged. Conveniently, according to something called "disengagement theory," which mainstream gerontology has largely dismissed as ageist and outdated, aging itself is on our side in this respect. For it leads us in various ways—socially, psychologically, and spiritually—to pull back from the cut and thrust of life and to keep the bigger picture in our minds. Whatever else it involves, wisdom is about keeping one's perspective. As my father would say, when he'd sit atop the hill above the house we lived in growing up and gaze out across the fields, it's about taking "the long view" of things. It's about not committing too quickly to a particular version of what's going on and where things are headed, for our stories of where things are headed invariably determine our feelings. In other words, our emotions always have narrative roots. If I'm sad or mad or glad in the face of a given situation, then chances are it's because I've interpreted that situation in terms of a storyline to which sadness or madness or gladness is a sensible response. Change the storyline and you change the emotion, which is, at bottom, what therapists—like Barbara, perhaps—help us to do when we're wrestling with a condition like depression. Yet our tendency is to totalize, to let what's happening in the present, positive or negative, dominate our sense of things and thereby rule our mood.

Wisdom is about keeping our stories open, not drawing conclusions in advance, not assuming we know how things will turn out, since the bald truth is that we *don't* know and we *can't* know. One of my mother's most frequently employed expressions is "you never know." In this respect, wisdom is about *not* knowing. More to the point, it's about being *okay* with not knowing.

Our current age, however, seems obsessed with knowledge, and obsessed with knowledge for knowledge's sake. "Where is the wisdom we have lost in knowledge?" laments the poet, and "Where is the knowledge we have lost in information?" To be fair, we know an awful lot of things that we never knew before, about atoms and galaxies, about diseases and DNA—the list goes on—but we still don't know it all. Nor *can* we know it all. "The universe," observed famed astronomer, J. B. S. Haldane, "is not only queerer than we suppose, but queerer than we *can* suppose." All of our knowledge and all of our information, as proud of it as we may be and as impressed with ourselves for having gained it, is relative at best. What we think we know for sure today could easily, a thousand years from now, be judged the superstitious gropings of an ancient race. Wisdom lies in knowing that our knowledge is forever incomplete.

The same is true with self-knowledge. "Know thyself," the Oracle of Delphi advises. And surely such advice is sound, provided we accept that knowing ourselves is an open-ended endeavor. There is no end of things to learn, to discover, to realize, within ourselves, as is the case with reading great works of literature. "The story" has a beginning, middle, and end, to be sure, but there's no end whatever to the meanings we can draw from it. Its meaning is indeterminate. With our *life* stories, however, the meaning of things is less determinate still, for we are always in The Middle. The Beginning of our stories is a dim and distant memory, and The End can never quite be reached. We live and tell and make sense of "the story of my life" always from within it, never without. Thus, the full significance of any one experience or circumstance can never be discerned because we can never step outside of it and see it with its own distinct beginning and end. For each experience is organic, blending in with others before it and after. What is more, we are forever having to revise our understanding of "our story" as a whole, as new events are added to the plot. And it's not just the future that's thus open in this manner. So, too, is the past. Past experiences can always undergo reworking, can always be re-membered. The heartache, the breakup, the layoff, the trauma, the missed opportunity, can turn out in retrospect to be the best thing that ever happened. We never know. While, yes, the past itself cannot be changed, our interpretation of it, or what we make of it in memory and imagination—which is ultimately what matters——can always be re-storied. "It's never too late to have a happy childhood," our therapist is wise to say.

Is what's happening in my life today—my partner bidding me adieu, a hurricane flattening my home, my doctor informing me that the test results have come back positive—the *whole* story? Or is it but a single event, whose significance has yet to be discerned? Sadly, as we enter our later years especially, rather than cleave to the long view of things, we can be tempted to assume that our story is all but over, that no new characters or episodes will figure in it, no new themes or chapters are apt to open up, that its ending is a foregone conclusion. Narrative gerontologists call this *narrative foreclosure*.

The opposite of narrative foreclosure is narrative openness, which means seeing that, where our life stories are concerned, things can always change. It means seeing that there's more to our story than we reckoned, that re-genre-ation, so to speak, is always a possibility. It means seeing that what might seem today an utter tragedy may, in hindsight, turn out to be a critical (if painful) juncture in the overall adventure of our life. And narrative openness means openness to how the ups and downs and ins and outs that figure in the fabric of a given day are ultimately unique. Never before in the history of the universe has the exact same arrangement occurred, certainly not with our own unique consciousness aware of it. As such—if we have the eyes to see and ears to hear—it can yield fresh new revelations ... into Life and Love, Grace and Truth, Ourselves. Despite the feeling we may default to that it's "the same old, same old," this new day is truly new. "This is the day that the Lord God hath made," exclaims the Psalmist; "let us rejoice and be glad therein."

As Yankees catcher Yogi Berra is famed for saying: "It ain't over till it's over." But is anything ever really *over*? Scholars have written about the ambiguity of "endings" in literature itself. For in some imagined world beyond the book, the land of Happy-Ever-After maybe, the story still goes on. Journalists know that today's top stories don't actually end so much as they fade from our awareness while the spotlight shifts swiftly and surely to the latest stories instead. From front page to back page to no page at all, they fade so much that they become fodder for historians, who for their part know that no version of the past is ever final but can always be superseded by a fuller, broader take on things. Astronomers deliberate on whether our universe could conclude some day in a Big Crunch. But even if it does, will this truly be The End, so they debate, or merely the prelude to another Big Bang, and so on and so forth, ad infinitum? For their part, scientists and theologians alike have questioned whether death is actually The End or simply a transition to some other realm where the lines between life and non-life, matter and energy, time and space, are so fuzzy as to be irrelevant. In this connection, what gerontologist, Leonard Hayflick, says on the question of "How old are you—really?" is worth hearing. Commenting on how Nature is about nothing if not a perpetual recycling of elements, he writes:

> If all but a few of the molecules in all of yourselves have turned over, then you are literally a different person today. ... All of your molecules ... are composed of more fundamental units called atoms, most of which have been the same since

our planet formed. You and I simply represent unique rear-rangements of ancient atoms that are themselves billions of years old. We are really composed of billion year atoms; we might actually claim to be immortal! In that sense we are all billion-year-olds no matter when we were born, and celebrating birthdays is absurd.

Talk about taking the long view of things. Talk about putting things in perspective. Talk about keeping our stories open. Surely the poor farmer would be pleased ...

Maybe yes, maybe no.

CHAPTER 9

Hansel and Gretel

BARBARA

Hansel and Gretel are the children of a poor woodcutter in medieval Germany. There is a great famine, and the children's stepmother, realizing that there is not enough food for all four of them, talks her husband into taking the children into the woods and abandoning them there, so that the two adults may have enough food to survive. After the parents have gone to bed, the boy surreptitiously runs out and gathers as many white pebbles as he can, and then returns to his room.

The next day, as they walk far into the woods, Hansel carefully leaves a trail of pebbles. After their parents abandon them, Hansel and Gretel follow the trail back home. The stepmother is furious but undeterred. She sends them to bed that night and locks the door to prevent further pebble-gathering. The following morning, the family again walks far into the woods. Hansel takes a slice of bread and leaves a trail of breadcrumbs; however, the crumbs are eaten by birds, so that there is no trail to follow when the children are again abandoned by the adults. Hansel and Gretel are lost.

After several days, the children come upon a large cottage built of gingerbread. The famished children begin to eat the roof, when the door opens and an old woman comes out and invites them in. She feeds them and puts them to bed, where they sleep gratefully. In the morning, though, the woman—in reality, a dreadful old witch—cackles with delight at her catch: a lovely little boy who will be delicious once he is fattened up a bit, and a little girl to do the housework. The witch throws Hansel into a cage and stuffs him with food to fatten him up, while Gretel is given just enough food to keep her alive and able to do the work. Realizing the plan, Gretel tries to convince the witch that Hansel is remaining stubbornly thin; but finally, the witch decides Hansel is fat enough. So she prepares the oven to cook him, and then figures she is hungry enough to eat Gretel, too. She coaxes Gretel to the open oven and prepares to push her in, but Gretel, figuring out what the woman's plan is, manages to push the crone into the oven, baking her to death. Gretel frees Hansel from the cage and the two find a hoard of jewels in the witch's house, which they take with them as they set off for home.

As they walk, all is unfamiliar, but they persevere. After a while, they come to a large lake, in which they see a white duck swimming. They call to her and ask her to take them across to the other side, which she does. After they cross the lake, they recognize familiar woods, and come upon their father's house. They arrive home to hear that their stepmother has died and the father has been miserable, missing his children. They live happily ever after.

Hansel and Gretel is basically a horrific story, somewhat redeemed by a relatively cheery ending. In medieval Germany, periodic famines did result in families abandoning children to forage by themselves in the forest when food ran out at home.

The tale might have served to reassure both children and parents of survival even if worse came to worst.

Older readers today might be reminded of our personal "coming of age" history. We might feel that we, too, had been forced out into the world before we were ready, and that college, or that first job, or the initial move away from home had been too daunting. Or perhaps we had never had a home with the essentials and had to forage as teenagers, with parents whose financial, physical, emotional, drug, or other problems precluded them from giving us a nourishing home environment. Parental death or serious illness, or some other familial disruption or disaster, can throw children into premature self-sufficiency.

We may have found ourselves rueing our parents' inability to provide us with adequate resources to grow and thrive at home, and the anger—and possibly contempt—for our parents' failings may have been an abiding resentment throughout adulthood. We survived but, unlike Hansel and Gretel, may have suffered lasting harm from losing our protected nest too soon.

If, however, we are reading this from a perch in older adulthood, no matter how precarious things were—or still are—we, like Hansel and Gretel, have survived. We were able to surmount difficulties—maybe even near-fatal experiences—and, even if scarred, lived through danger and frailty. We have perhaps even thrived. It may be of use to acknowledge the inner resources that helped us, and the strengths and capabilities we developed along the way.

Perhaps, though, we were kept too long at home, not allowed to face life's challenges, but given the message that we were too little, or too young, too weak, or too inadequate in other ways to face the world on our own. We may envy the hardy, clever Hansel and Gretel, who are given the opportunity to develop their resourcefulness and grow in strength and confidence. We may resent the overprotective parents who hampered our growth.

Either way, we might—in the context of this story—acknowledge our ability to have tolerated whatever failures our parents may have demonstrated, and see their limitations through our older, more generous eyes. We may well have no idea of the ways in which they themselves went without the nourishment they needed—and did the best they could to survive and set us free. Maybe now, even after our parents' deaths, we can follow the children's example of offering their aging father the fruits of their adventures and their love.

This story of woefully inadequate parenting may bring, as well, some uncomfortable tinge of recognition that might be of use. Those of us who are parents might well recall when our children had to go out on their own, find their own path. This is rarely an easy time in family life, and the decision of timing is often fraught. If the pushes and pulls and ambivalence of adolescence were painful, or if the achievement of independence seemed to take forever, we might well have found ourselves reacting uncomfortably similarly to Hansel and Gretel's father and stepmother prior to the involuntary launch. We may feel we were inappropriately relieved when they left home. Did their presence interfere in what we wanted to do, or did the money spent to support them deprive us of things we wanted, or needed? Did we assume—or demand—their independence before they felt themselves ready to leave the nest?

Or, on the other hand, did we strive to keep them children, dreading their departure, unsure of what our life would be with such a big part of it removed? The story seems to suggest that the children, though facing daunting challenges, were, in fact, up to the task—and they triumphed. It is often easy to underestimate our children's strengths, or to rely too much on the personal gratification of their presence. Maybe our children's presence, and everyday concerns, enabled us to avoid our own vocational, personal, or marital challenges. Maybe we tried to convince our children, and ourselves, that their well-being would be improved by putting off independent living, while really it was we ourselves we were protecting. Either way, were we focused on their needs or our own? Being parents can seem, amidst its enormous pleasures, an unending series of fraught decisions whose outcomes are murky, often for years. An honest examination of some of these decisions might enable us to be grateful for what has turned out well—and perhaps to forgive ourselves for ways we handled things that were not ideal, but were the best we could do at the time. It's unlikely that many of us were as cravenly unloving as the father was initially, as self-centeredly cruel as the stepmother, or as sadistically murderous as the witch. Maybe our own parental imperfections can be understood and forgiven in this later season of our lives.

The adult women in the story are less sympathetic than the ultimately sweet, if ineffectual, father. Clearly, the stepmother is pretty cruel, abandoning the children. Maybe it's because she can't bear to see them starve to death, though leaving them to die by themselves seems particularly mean-spirited. But the witch is simply diabolical. She has candy to spare, and enough food to feed herself and Hansel well. But she gives Gretel almost nothing, and treats her meanly, and her feeding of Hansel is only to give herself more to devour later.

The witch seems the embodiment of the uncaring, often cruel world that lures us by promising wonderful treats, but cares nothing for us. We know individuals—and institutions—like this who flatter and use people but have no real concern for their well-being, even if they know don't actually murder and eat them! On the one hand, this is an aspect of the world which we, like the children, need to understand if we are not to be destroyed. We can be flattered into thinking that praise, promotions, money, and material acquisitions will make us happy, but those things can be fleeting and offer us no protection from the ultimate carelessness of the world. Many older people feel that they have been "eaten up" by the demands of career or the desire to maintain a certain lifestyle. (Perhaps an even greater danger is that we ourselves might have become a bit like the callous witch, presenting an alluring pretense, with little real concern for the "little ones" we try to bring into our orbit.) Age can be cruel in its stripping away of the trappings of a "good life," revealing the falseness of its tempting appearance. If we have succumbed to the temptation to live in a world of flashy facades, then we may find that aging, and our replacement by younger, more virile, prettier adherents of the philosophy of self-important materialism, can dethrone us mercilessly. Unlike the witch, though, we may be given an opportunity to re-evaluate our priorities, and learn to appreciate substance—in ourselves as well as others.

And what of the innocents? At the beginning of this story, the children are in quite a fraught situation. They cannot stay at home: there is a famine, and their household has food enough only for two. Either they starve, their parents starve, or one of each will starve. The parents have made a home; the children need to leave and either die or learn how to provide for themselves, regardless of how unappealing that is. The world is unknown and full of dangers, but after the second futile attempt to return home, it is clear that the children have to make the best of being on their own. And they do.

As we age, many of us feel the shock of being "thrown out" of our adult lives—by deaths of loved ones, by our own illnesses, by the leaving of grown children, or by retirement. Often, the departure of resident children precedes retirement from an outside job, so in many families, retirement is at least a two-step process. But in either case, the transition may be somewhat similar to that of our Hansel and Gretel: unsought, unwelcome, and unfamiliar. Although many people retire voluntarily—even eagerly—there is a sense, for most, of trepidation. Many plan for retirement and/or child-free living as a sort of full-time vacation: maybe a move—permanent or for several months a year—to a waterside community, or frequent long-distance travel. Maybe we immediately sign up for volunteer work, or classes at a nearby college. For some, full retirement comes as a shock: from full-speed ahead to a complete stop. Or from being a homemaker free to set a daily schedule, completely independently, to having a partner underfoot all day long. Even in the midst of planned, desired activities, retirement can be deeply unsettling, with so much of quotidian life suddenly gone. The sense that our life's work, which in important ways defined us, is finished can be profoundly disorienting, and many feel as if they are wandering around in a confusing forest, with no clear sense of purpose or solid grounding. We may rush toward the first thing that seems to offer sustenance and solace, only to find it as unfulfilling as a house of sugar.

There are other ways, too, that aging people can feel thrown out of their home and left to forage in a frightening, shocking wilderness. A spouse—or child, dear sibling, or best friend—may die, plunging us into a scary sense of isolation, and a keener awareness of our own vulnerability. We may become ill, and the consequences of that illness may include an unforeseen and troubling dependency. The loss of autonomy may "merely" be the result of poor eyesight, taking away our ability to drive at night. Or we may become functionally blind on a permanent basis. Hearing loss may diminish our lifelong joy of sharing meals in favorite restaurants—or, if more severe, our ability to socialize at all. Health problems may interfere, temporarily or permanently, with our ability to drive, let alone to walk.

Many, even when still healthy and independent, move to an elder-friendly environment, focused on forming new relationships with people of the same generation. Often, the move is to a community with available options designed to help with physical or cognitive decline. Such a transition, even when freely chosen, can be laden with fear and distaste for the possibility of being seen as less than adequate, or treated as children in an infantile environment.

There may be greater unwelcome and non-negotiable losses as well. The increasing difficulty in climbing stairs may necessitate a move from our home. We may become dependent more and more on others for our daily needs and have to relocate to some form of long-term care, well before we have any desire to relinquish our autonomy.

Even without such life-altering changes, we may face concerns about increasing constraints on our lives. Some need not worry about food, housing, or medical expenses; but even if there are no financial concerns and we are healthy and active, we know that medical concerns become increasingly common as we age, and we see friends and family beginning to deteriorate. The future, far from clear, is filled with uncertainty. So it is for Hansel and Gretel, too, as they suddenly lose their home and, with it, all the familiar comforts, and they face fearsome and unknown challenges. Will they be able to succeed in making a life in the unfamiliar wilderness, where enemies and sudden, possibly fatal, cataclysms could appear at any time?

How are we to overcome the losses, and potential aridity, of elderhood? One of the needs—and, when satisfied, comforts—we see in this story is that of companionship. Hansel and Gretel have, and value, each other, and each has gifts and abilities that are essential to their joint success—in the forest, at the crone's house, on the way home. Alone, neither could triumph over the witch, but together they are able to maintain hope and work together. Even their mutuality, though, is not enough for them. Instead of staying in the dead witch's house together, with its material comforts and jewels, food, and anything else they might desire, Hansel and Gretel want a fuller relational life. Their love of their father is what gives them a purpose in life: reunion with him. Most people of any age want some sort of community or companionship. Many older people reconnect with family, or begin new relationships, strengthened and changed by life's ups and downs.

Still, having faced—and perhaps, to some degree, surmounted—the daunting challenges of adjusting to life with ineradicable limitations, we come, in time, to face the ultimate challenge of our trip to, or through, death. We foresee a future with unwelcome uncertainty, just as Hansel and Gretel, having surmounted the dangers of the murderous witch, face the unfamiliar challenges of a looming lake. Perhaps the lake hints at another sort of homecoming: not just the adaptations to a new way of elder-life, but to the possibility of a spiritual journey, too—a journey through the waters of death.

During the late Middle Ages in Europe, when these sorts of stories probably developed, people did not swim recreationally, and large bodies of water were not playgrounds but perilous environments. Anticipating crossing over a large lake would not have been like planning a quiet paddle to a nearby islet for a picnic, but contemplating a dangerous foray into the unknown. As we look at the journeys of later life, we too may envision our final journey into the frightening, bottomless unknown. We may struggle with the prospect of acquiescing to a trip not of our own choosing. We may wonder whether all that we've accumulated here will be seen as dross and render us inadequate at our destination. We have no detailed map of what is ahead and so we may face the terror of the absolute unknown. Will we find ourselves drowning without any happy reunion? For many there is a hope that the other side of the lake will bring us to reunions of perfect joy. We may hope that the gifts we have acquired through hardship, perseverance, love, wit, and effort will remain with us throughout the trip and be useful wherever we arrive. Or we may hope that they and the pain that attended their learning will have fallen off as we ride the duck back to the home of all that is good.

One of the gifts of the story of Hansel and Gretel is that there is no sappy denial of the real suffering of this world. There is no one in the story except the children (and the duck) who is not guilty of terrible cruelty. There is no one who is able to avoid significant misfortune. Hardworking laborer, resentful overburdened mother, innocent child, rich witch—none is spared. But the story suggests that the suffering—and our own inadequacies—may not be the final word. This earthly life might end, and a rebirth through transformative waters might lead us (back) to a new, unending life. Maybe we return to our creator, who rejoiced in the gifts we have found and now give back, and who welcomes us into that loving life which has no end.

CHAPTER 10

Jesus Calms the Storm

ANDY

After a long day aboard a boat preaching to crowds on the shore, Jesus tells his disciples that he wants to go to the other side of the Sea of Galilee. A furious squall arises on the voyage, which terrifies the crew. The tempest apparently does not disturb Jesus, who is fast asleep at the stern. When he wakes up, he calms the storm, and asks his disciples why they were so afraid—was it lack of faith? Still terrified, the disciples ponder what has occurred and ask each other who Jesus is.

The story of Jesus calming the sea and then questioning his disciples' faith is told in all three synoptic Gospels. The details are richest in Mark's account, which is the version interpreted here (Mark 4:35-39). The summary, though, does not convey the drama—of fear pitted against faith—a transformational event upon which we, too, can meditate.

For a year, a motley group of ordinary men had been following this itinerant teacher; they (and other witnesses) probably had grown accustomed to him being constantly on the go. The disciples watched with awe as he cared for the sick and needy, and as he healed widows and the blind who prayerfully approached him. Even so, they still did not fully ascertain the depths of their calling.

In a sense, they were no different from the crowd on the shore that day who listened to Jesus, sitting aboard one of his disciple's boats, relate the parable of the mustard seed. Some Jews and Gentiles who gathered listened attentively. Others were curious or cynical observers. After speaking for hours, Jesus decided to leave the crowds behind, "to go over to the other side" of the Sea of Galilee. This was his first incursion into pagan territory, where he intended to spread Good News.

The boat transporting Jesus was big enough to hold twelve people. Some sailors aboard had survived shipwrecks—harrowing experiences that did not overcome fearful memories, especially as dusk turned into night. Mark describes this body of water as dangerously full of swift currents and sea monsters. Perhaps realizing that "there were also other boats with him" calmed nerves, for the voyagers were not alone; they could take refuge in numbers. Being part of a convoy was reassuring, since some fellow travelers heading across the sea had often made it to safety without mishap.

Jesus, exhausted, falls asleep on a cushion. Revealing the teacher's human nature, Mark notes that Jesus does not volunteer for a night watch; he wants to be left alone, undisturbed. Nonetheless, if necessary, the disciples doubtless think that Jesus will tend to his flock—in the generous, caring way that he does everything.

Then suddenly, out of nowhere, a storm erupts. Winds sweep through narrow gorges. Waves break overhead, swamping the deck. More than a few of the sailors and passengers have survived storms at sea earlier in life. Their collective memories do not diminish the trauma at hand, however. Carpenters have patched up the boat, but with its tall sail and shallow keel, it can be quickly capsized in raging waters. The sailors deftly shift the vessel's position. Yet Jesus stays asleep, seemingly oblivious to the furious squall.

Terror naturally grips the disciples and virtually everyone else on board. Will dragons eat or death sweep away the passengers whose bodies are chilled by freezing waters and unrelenting gales? Those trying to adjust the sail grow sore, testy, and frustrated. Men are vomiting, just as Rembrandt portrayed in his masterpiece, "Christ in the Storm on the Sea of Galilee." Some try to displace their fears, I imagine, wondering whether the Son of Man is a trickster testing mortals' will. Amazingly, he stays asleep amid the tempest, ignoring cries for help. He cannot be roused to offer an encouraging word or say a prayer to quell the utter desperation around him.

But wait: Jesus is getting up and standing tall. The Son of Man rebukes the wind and calms the water—"Quiet!" he commands. "Be still!" The forces of Nature become completely subdued. Then Mark offers a penultimate verse to the account: "Why are you so afraid?" Jesus asks. "Have you still no faith?" Shaken and terrified by what has transpired, his followers silently wonder about this man with miraculous power.

I have heard many sermons about relying on faith to dispel doubts and fears. Preachers' pleas for courage and patience do not assuage dreadful memories of how poorly I often dealt with rejection in high school, much less related to assaults on my pride thereafter. I vividly recall worrying the morning of my first wedding about how much I lacked in aspiring to be a loving husband and supportive father. Professionally competitive and insecure, I took steps up the career ladder suffering pain, incapable of embracing the gain. And after teaching gerontology courses for four decades, I have difficulty adjusting to retirement. Once I busily imparted sage counsel and practical wisdom. Now I am grappling with questions that I had rarely asked students or myself. On top of unresolved issues, novel late-life challenges arise: should my second wife and I move closer to our children and grandchildren, selfishly scouting out assisted-care facilities before we are too frail to do otherwise?

I know that some of life's transitions go according to expectations—some plans proving better or worse than anticipated. "Life is like a box of chocolates," opines Forrest Gump, "You never know what you're gonna get." Furthermore, I have made enough mistakes in moving ahead to realize that uncertainties (conscious or otherwise) shadow fears that I try to deflect or dismiss. It is more terrifying than unnerving to brace for threats to my well-being. Like those sailors and voyagers in the midst of the storm, I wonder why Jesus sleeps. Like them, I am often at sea in dire straits; I too am disinclined to trust in God's miraculous ways.

Mark offers readers another tack. He invites me to explore how I approximate the disciples' spiritual bonds to Nature, to others, and to God. Faith does not magically silence fears and doubts, but his account of that journey across the Sea of Galilee is more than a wake-up call. Turmoil and tempests test our mettle. Threatened by turbulent winds and chilling waves, my first impulse is to do whatever is necessary to survive. When wits and brawn fail to save the sinking ship, I puke while I prepare to fall overboard. Where are you, Jesus? I thought that following you would lead me to safety.

Painful, scary, chaotic crises bring out the good, the bad, and the ugly in me. Ultimately, I associate my fear of death with my fear of God—an analogy difficult to acknowledge and articulate in a secular era. Frightening transitions potentially occasion moments of spiritual maturity in which soul mates assess end-of-life journeys. Often the exercise yields mixed results. It is distressing to reflect intentionally on what we have done and what we have failed to accomplish. Such reckoning may prompt us to exaggerate successes and justify mistakes that still might be rectified. Prideful perfectionism can disconnect us from loving others and communing with God.

For me, engaging in life review arouses dread more often than peace, particularly as I imagine Jesus rebuking me for having so little faith, hope, or trust. Will he confront me as a force of Nature, wallowing in self-pity and oblivious to the power bestowed on the Son of Man who was the Son of God? Am I destined to survive one storm only to face suffering and torment in the next? Maybe the wind died down and the sea became completely calm because they were not just ordered to become still; they were humbled into accepting their place in the great chain of Being.

Mark never seems to provide narratives with neat endings. I might surmise that the account of "Jesus calms the storm" comes too early in his Gospel, but he concludes his Resurrection narrative with ellipses ... . Rather than bemoan the vicissitudes of growing older, perhaps I should meditate in solitary stillness. If the tempests of life signify that bad things happen to everybody (including those on spiritual journeys), then in calm I can dimly awaken to the miracle of God's presence with me. Grace may yet empower me to stay awake. I can choose to accept that the forces of Nature are awesome and awful—even unto death where, we hope, we shall encounter unexpected and unwarranted bliss and peace.

CHAPTER 11

The Emperor's New Clothes

BILL

Two weavers promise an emperor a new suit of clothes that they say is invisible to anyone who is stupid, incompetent, or otherwise unfit for their position. In reality, the swindlers make no clothes at all, making everyone believe that the clothes are invisible only to them. When the emperor parades before his subjects in his new "clothes," no one dares to say that they do not see any clothes on him for fear they will be deemed stupid. Finally a child cries out, "But he isn't wearing anything at all!"

Once upon a time, in a land far away, there was an emperor who lived his life on a lavish scale. According to no less an authority than himself, he was the smartest man in the world, a genius no less, and a very stable one at that. A veritable one-man show, he loved the most expensive possessions, stayed at the glitziest hotels, and consorted with the flashiest, most audacious individuals. His favorites, however, were fellow emperors. He envied the unchallenged sway that they held over their own people and he yearned to be just like them.

He had a particular love—though "love" is not the word—for sycophants. He insisted that his court be filled with them. He adored the flattery they showed him, the way they acclaimed his every whim, as self-serving as those whims so often were. His courtiers flattered him, however, not because they loved him in return. They flattered him because they were afraid of him. They were afraid of him because they knew that if they questioned his genius in the tiniest measure, they would fall from his favor as swiftly as could be—like others before them—and, just as swiftly, be out of a job. Very wisely, then, they kept their mouths shut and pretended that everything was fine. Besides, compared to conditions under previous emperors, the kingdom was once again great, its economy bursting at the seams. So their job, they fervently felt, was to let him do *his* job, which meant letting him be him.

The emperor, however, was no ordinary emperor, for he was both a weaver and a merchant as well, not to mention a master of the art of making deals, very clever deals that profited few if any but himself. How convenient, then, and how economical as far as our little story is concerned, for he was an emperor, a weaver, and a swindler all at once. Three for the price of one. A wonderful deal indeed!

Day after day, he sat weaving away, tailoring the truth to suit his own needs, and spinning a magical brand of wool with which, not just his courtiers, but all manner of god-fearing folk could fashion the most marvelous veils to wrap around their heads and seal their brains in a cozy cocoon. And as they pulled the precious tissue across their eyes, then—*Abracadabra!*—it shielded them from the havoc he was wreaking throughout the land, dividing and conquering wherever he could and, strand by strand, unravelling the fabric of fairness and decency that once held their kingdom together.

Happily, not all of his subjects were bamboozled in this manner. Many—though not as many as you'd think—kept their eyes wide open and refused to rally round the giant bowl of Kool-Aid from which everyone else so mindlessly drank. They could see how transparent the emperor really was, and see through to the raw, unbridled ego that he paraded so brazenly before them, day in and day out, trailing behind him a cloud of lawsuits and lies. One by one—a senator here, a whistleblower there, a late-night comedian, a palace employee turned tell-all author, a teenage environmentalist from a faraway land—they stepped forth from the crowd. "He is no genius," they each called out. "Nor is he the least bit stable. He is no benevolent leader with our best interests in mind, but a narcissistic buffoon. He is bad news. Bad for the environment, bad for the poor, bad for all concerned. And he is bad, too, for our most esteemed institutions, as one by one he turns them on their heads, alienating our allies every chance he gets, and ruining our name around the globe."

"No, no, NO!" the emperor roared back. "A thousand times, no!" he bellowed at these insolent detractors. "I am not bad news, not fake news; I am good news, the best news ever ..."

And so, we see how transparent our little tale—so funny yet so frightening—has become. Clearly, a number of the stories that we're looking into in this book beg, like this one, to be read on more than a personal level alone. So, having gotten this silly spoof of it out of my system, let me turn to other, subtler, yet equally serious, ways that the situation it sets out is sadly true to life.

Swindlers, con-men, scammers, anyone who cruises on the edge of outright criminality—these have always been with us, if not always on so imperial a scale. But in every sector—politics and religion, commerce and finance, education and entertainment—they can certainly be found. Scarcely a sector of society is immune. From televangelists to telemarketers, from movie moguls to movie stars to celebrities of every sort, there are those whose sole goal is to get something for nothing: to pull the wool over our eyes, to sell us a bill of goods, to dazzle us with smoke and mirrors, to lure us into the big tent at the county fair for the price of our hard-earned allowance to behold the world's smallest horse or fattest man, to take advantage of us in whatever way they can. Not just the weak and unwitting, but the rich and the privileged, the young and the old, and everyone in between.

The aged—like the three of us—are especially easy prey ... to that "nice young woman," for instance, who calls to tell you that your credit card has unfortunately expired and that if you will only just give her your banking information, then, presto, she'll make the problem go away. Or to the man in the shiny blue truck with the sign that says "A-One Roofing" who knocks at your door and graciously offers to replace the shingles that flew off during the hurricane last autumn, if only you'll make a down payment of $500 until he can return with his crew the following week to do the job. Or to the thick, enticing-looking envelope with all manner of colorful flyers for nifty things you have no need of, that contains a letter with your very own name at the top of it, informing you that, wonder of wonders, you've been chosen from thousands of others to be among the top 100 contestants to win the grand prize of $10,000,000, if only you'll send in a check for $10 to secure your place on the list.

My father fell victim, sort of, to a scheme like this in his late eighties and early nineties. Each week, he faithfully ordered an assortment of gadgets and trinkets that the flyers described, things neither he nor my mother needed in the least and wrote out the check to keep his name on the list, for a total of up to $30 or $40 of their hard-earned savings every time. Although he confided in me that, at his age, he and Mother didn't really need the $10 million, his children and grandchildren could still benefit from it, or from the $1000 per month for life that the bonanza could supposedly be paid out in. The man was no fool, and on some level he knew perfectly well that, yes, the entire thing was a sting; that, send as much money as he might, he would never, ever win. But as he explained the matter to me, it meant that there would always be something to look forward to in the mail. What is more, it helped him pass the time, pawing through the flyers, filling out the forms, sealing the self-addressed envelope, and mailing it all back.

This whole business of willed ignorance, which Andersen lays bare for us so wittily, as the emperor parades before his people in the buff, is both amusing and revealing. It's the collective illusion—like "culture" as a whole, you could argue, entails—that we buy into as Reality, as "the way things are"—even when we know full well, from the course we took in anthropology at college or from spending some serious time in a radically different country, that there are several other ways as well. It's the business of knowing and yet, simultaneously and intentionally, *not* knowing. It's living with your eyes wide shut.

People who work in business or bureaucracy of any sort are familiar with this phenomenon. They live it every day. The boss is a jerk—everyone knows it—but he is, after all, the boss, so you make nice to his face and keep your grousings to yourself. Or with a wink here or a raised eyebrow there, you hint at them slyly to your office mates beside the coffee urn, and then vent them more freely over drinks after hours. Otherwise, you go with the flow, mind your P's and Q's, and keep up appearances, lest you be branded a trouble-maker, get passed over for that promotion, or lose your job entirely. You say one thing on the surface while meaning quite another underneath. "Yes, sir. I agree with you, sir. Lovely tie you're wearing, sir. Have yourself a lovely evening, sir."

We're talking here about open secrets, which can be par for the course, of course, in small communities everywhere, like the one where I grew up. "Everyone knows" that the mayor is running around with the banker's wife, and the owner of the hot dog stand is dealing drugs to teens. And they can be rampant in the church, where, for instance, everyone knows the bishop is covering up that scandal from two decades back. Everyone knows, yet no one says a word, nor does anything about it. No one steps up to blow the whistle, pull the plug, and demand an inquiry because ... why rock the boat? We'll only end up hurting ourselves, shooting ourselves in the foot. Let someone else deal with the matter, some other time. Or they are at play in our relationship to Nature, where everyone knows that the forests are being raped—like the woods that surround me (or used to) where I live—with only isolated attempts being made at reforestation, at restoring habitats for critters that are being displaced at an accelerating pace. Yet most of us, me for one, do little or nothing to bring the pillaging to an end.

Our capacity to cope with cognitive dissonance, as it's called, knows few limitations. It might well be the hallmark of the human mind. The chickadees and squirrels that come to my feeders (because they have fewer and fewer options perhaps?) haven't an inkling what cognitive dissonance is, of course, nor the remotest ability, like the Queen in Wonderland, to believe six impossible things before breakfast. What they see—the birdseed in front of them or the hawk making circles in the sky—is what is real, what concerns them most, the thing they believe at the time. And they lack totally the talent for that special brand of cognitive dissonance known as self-deception, which for us as *homo sapiens*, may be the normal pathology of everyday life.

A chronic puzzle for philosophers, self-deception is the paradoxical state of being mindful, on one level, of certain qualities we possess but are not especially proud of, yet which, on another level, we make a semi-conscious decision to ignore. It concerns deeds that we've done which we wish very much we hadn't, yet we comport ourselves as if that were indeed the case. In fact, so convincing is our act that, for all intents and purposes, the deeds are stricken from memory's record—a record that is patchy at best. Self-deception concerns corners of our past that we turn a blind eye to, until they turn up to dog us on the campaign trail, or in a session with our therapist, or in a new relationship that forces us, like it or lump it, toward heightened self-understanding.

I like what Florida Scott-Maxwell, writing in her eighties, has to say: "When you truly possess all you have been and done, which may take some time, you are fierce with reality." When you possess—when you own, when you own *up* to—the good, the bad, and the ugly in your personality and your life; when you engage, with courage, in the process of life review that psychologists say is essential to achieving an internal integrity in later life, then you are, if not fierce with reality, then at least facing up to it, staring it squarely in the eye, in ways you haven't done before. Not shrinking back, not retreating behind your accomplishments, behind the usual illusions, personal or collective, not going along with the crowd, but calling a spade a spade. Like you did, more naturally, as a child, pure of heart, eyes wondering and wide—*Why? What's that? How come?*—and without a "self" sufficiently firmed up to be capable of self-deception in the first place.

I wonder … could there be a second innocence that parallels the innocence of childhood, one which, if we let it, comes naturally with age, with a lifetime of experience, reflected on and wrestled with, at last beneath our belts?

Some psychologists claim that personal development is a matter of progressive dis-illusionment—not in the cynical sense that we typically understand that term, where experience makes us jaded and sour—but in the sense of seeing through the assortment of false assumptions (from *Santa Claus is Real* to *Father Knows Best*) that hold us back from full maturity and blind us to the light. I mean stage by stage, lesson learned by lesson learned, facing our humanity and mortality, facing full-on the life that we've lived and the person we've become. I mean the scales that have built up, from years of slogging through the fog of life, falling from our eyes and us breaking through at last to where we can see clearly what is real, what is true.

"A long life makes me feel nearer truth," Scott-Maxwell also notes, summing up neatly the state of heart that I'm envisioning here, "yet it won't go into words, so how can I convey it? I can't, and I want to. I want to tell people approaching and perhaps fearing age that it is a time of discovery. If they say, 'Of what?' I can only answer, 'We must each find out for ourselves, otherwise it won't be discovery.'"

It's a small child, of course, who turns things around in the end by voicing out loud what everyone else was seeing and thinking but didn't dare admit. "Unless you change and become like little children," the Good Book advises ... The innocence of little children, the freedom from guile, the wide-eyed openness to exactly what's in front of us—might this not be part of what, with age, we could recover?

CHAPTER 12

Sleeping Beauty

BARBARA

In a small kingdom long ago, seven fairies have been invited to a party for the newborn royal princess. After six have presented their gifts (beauty, wit, grace, goodness, etc.), an eighth fairy arrives. Old and living in an otherwise empty tower, she has been forgotten. Enraged at the slight, she gives her "gift": an enchantment that the girl will, when a teenager, prick her finger on a spinning wheel and die. The fairy who has not yet given her gift is, like the others, horrified. She tries to undo the evil fairy's curse, but is only able to change it: the girl will prick her finger but will only be asleep for a hundred years, at which point she will be awakened by the kiss of a prince. The distraught king orders that all spinning wheels be removed, and life goes on.

When the girl is about fifteen, she is wandering around the castle and comes upon an old spinster, overlooked by the original order to remove all spinning wheels. Interested in this novelty, the princess asks to try the wheel and, her finger pricked, she falls asleep. The spinster alerts the rest of the castle, and the girl is moved to bed. The good fairy is summoned and, in order to avoid

110

the princess's awakening to solitude, she puts all the inhabitants of the castle in a similar sleep. The forest around the castle becomes impenetrably dense—princes hearing rumors of the situation try unsuccessfully to penetrate the woods and brambles. A hundred years pass. Another prince arrives and hears the tale of the sleeping princess; he is able to get through the thorns, brambles, and dense overgrowth. He enters the castle and roams around until he finds the princess, whose beauty delights him. He kisses her and she wakens. The castle's other inhabitants awake, as well, and life resumes. The prince and princess wed.

The two oldest people in this story are intriguing. Both the evil fairy and the spinster are overlooked. One is completely innocent, and her role is tragic. All the spinsters are sought out and their livelihood destroyed. Presumably they find other employment in the castle. But this one woman isn't found, even as the king demands the scouring of the place for all spinning wheels. How invisible she is! Years later, the princess comes upon her by accident. The spinster calls for help but is unable to avert tragedy. First she is ignored, although apparently in clear view. Then she is, completely innocently, the cause of great calamity. By contrast, the evil fairy, enraged at having been forgotten, does her best—which is a lot—to punish everyone.

How many older people, sitting in plain view, continuing to work, to write papers, to do their job well, have become invisible? It often doesn't seem to matter how we were viewed before: whether we were the critical old crone or the eager-to-please aging person, we are still overlooked as the younger generations take over. Ranting and raging doesn't return us to the leadership or other roles we once had. Neither does passive acquiescence. The world moves on, and it does so with different, younger leadership. How we face this is a critical issue in our aging. Some simply deny the reality and make every effort to continue as before. Most people probably have a variety of reactions, from the rage of the evil fairy to the passive solitude of the overlooked spinster who ignores the reality around her and continues doing her job, despite the fact that it has been declared unnecessary. We know the parents who seem not to recognize that their children are grown, have become functioning adults, and often make decisions that differ from those of their parents. We know the corporate executives whose staunch views, based on their long experience, are increasingly dismissed by their younger colleagues.

Once we see ourselves, even faintly, in the resentful old crone or lonesome spinster, we can begin to struggle more creatively to find ways to heal our loss. There are still real gifts we have, even though our old workplace, or even family life, might not be the place to use them anymore. But there may be other outlets; and other, yet unused, gifts we might discover once we deal with the hurt and loss of our former position.

Or maybe we see ourselves in the king. His horror and grief must be great: just as he is celebrating a long-awaited gift, it is threatened and wounded. He races to do what he can, trying to shield his daughter from all possible danger. Like all parents, though, he is incapable of providing absolute safety. If you are a parent—or teacher, or supervisor, or other guardian of a developing person—you have faced the Scylla and Charybdis of protecting, on the one hand, and allowing for the development of self-sufficiency, on the other. We might have been overprotective, or too lax. And we may well have seen the negative effects of one or the other extreme. Might we acknowledge ways in which we were unhelpful? And might we, then, forgive ourselves?

Maybe we could even be able to recognize ourselves in the good fairy, who mitigates the spell in the beginning, and later amends it to provide protection and solace for the princess when she finally awakens. Maybe we have made efforts—or can now do so—to modify and ease situations for others. While the good fairy will not be the star of the show, it is her kindness and concern which ease the harsh realities faced by the major characters. Maybe you can see yourself in this very important but often overlooked role—a role that grandparents often play, as do caring parish members or other unassuming, caring friends behind-the-scenes.

Happier times return a hundred years later, with our hardy, determined prince. He struggles mightily to save the princess, and does so. This prince is young, strong, intrepid, determined, and susceptible to female beauty. Even before he sees her beauty, though, he is seduced by the mysterious hidden castle and its fabled sleeping princess. What motivates such chivalry? Maybe he really doesn't have that much to do at home, and is ready to move into adulthood and new responsibilities. It's certainly possible that there are few available, appropriate princesses in the area, and performing this challenging feat might be his way of both acquiring an appropriate partner and proving his mettle as a future king.

Although such knight-errantry may seem far from our culture, there are still challenges through which young people demonstrate their adult capacities. (And often undertake actions which their elders would deem foolhardy, such as attempting to get through a forest that's been impenetrable for decades.) Successful completion of the various quests and challenges of college, or of first jobs, may serve to help navigate the challenging move from childhood to adulthood. We ourselves may have undertaken various coming-of-age quests. We may still be trying to prove that we're adults, comparing ourselves with our parents—even if they are long dead. What challenges have we set before our children, demanding that they "prove" themselves before we will agree to treat them as adults?

One character in this story whom we have not yet discussed is Sleeping Beauty herself. Probably one reason is that she, as a person, seems almost immaterial to the story. At the beginning, she's an infant. We do have an image of her fifteen years later, as a curious, somewhat adventuresome young woman, eager to explore areas of the castle that she's never seen and attempt new activities, like spinning cloth. This curious young woman then disappears for a hundred years, at the end of which time she is awakened by a prince. She talks with him and then marries him. Not a robust picture of a person, here.

Many people have commented on Sleeping Beauty's passivity—in fact, it is her unconsciousness that is the center of the story. Her mother, too, is presented as pretty much a nonentity: she is described only as having wished for her daughter's birth and then, after the girl is put to sleep, having kissed her. It is the good fairy, not the mother, who expresses concern about how Sleeping Beauty will react when she awakens in a hundred years, alone. Is this kind of beautiful passivity what "good" women are still called to embody? The story has three major types of women: beautiful, privileged women with limited personality or initiative (Sleeping Beauty and her mother); evil women with a certain amount of power (the evil fairy); and the occasional woman who is caring and has some, though limited, ability to make a difference in the world (the good fairy and, in her generosity toward Sleeping Beauty, the spinster).

Men in this tale expect to be capable of great derring-do: for example, penetrating the impenetrable forest and undoing the fairy's curse. And when the king is unable to do the latter, he accepts the curse, unwelcome though it is, because it is not his limitations that have failed to undo it; it must be that it is ordained by unchangeable fate.

While this worldview may still be prevalent, there has in many places been some movement toward greater gender parity. Women are often, now, lauded as much for their professional capability as for their attractiveness. And men are more frequently permitted to express feelings—of, say, depression or fear—rather than always be stalwart and strong. What has your experience been with this? Did you grow up with strong gender-based expectations? How have they fit with your own gifts, abilities, and interests? How has this affected you, and your relationships with women and men?

The crux of this story, of course, is the curse. It is made abundantly clear that this curse—of near-death—is in no way due to any fault or misdeed on the part of Sleeping Beauty. She is an infant when she is burdened by the curse, and the intent is not merely unconsciousness, but death. Sleeping Beauty is cursed because her parents have forgotten to invite the crone to the christening. The baby, in a real sense, is used as a weapon against the parents, who are predictably distraught. And there is an added cruelty to the spell: it will not take place until an unspecified future time. The malicious fairy ensures that the king and queen will live in an agony of fear until the day the girl pricks her finger. We can certainly imagine that, even with the king's efforts to avoid the curse by banning spindles, he and his wife have had enough belief in curses that they live under this cloud of worry for the fifteen years before it is realized.

In Sleeping Beauty's case, the fear seems to have been the worst of it. Once she pricks her finger and the entire palace goes to sleep, there is no fear, no pain—just sleep, until the joy of the awakening. Many of us have probably succumbed to the temptation to live in fear of what the future may bring. For some of us, anxiety has been a lifelong, generalized companion. For others of us, fears have changed over time, morphing from fears of academic or social failures into fears for children's well-being and/or professional concerns. As we age, many of us increasingly fear illness, suffering, material or cognitive losses, to say nothing of death itself.

The curse of fear and anxiety: have I gotten rid of all the spindles, or might one still exist? What disaster might destroy the savings I count on for retirement and possible illness and nursing expenses?

What will happen to my children/spouse/pets? How will I handle the pain and the diminishment of aging and illness? Of course, the vicissitudes of aging, illness, and death can be difficult and painful, and the fact that the specifics of our future challenges are unknown can add to our concerns. But there seems a particular irony in adding anticipatory fear to the unavoidable challenges. Have we ourselves fallen into that? How might we—through realistic planning, clear-sighted acknowledgment of the possibilities, and other preparations—alleviate what fear we have?

Certainly an honest examination, too, of our beliefs about death might be of use. What, truly, do I believe about death? Is there an afterlife? Does its nature depend on my moral worthiness? Is there something I might do about that? Do I believe there is no afterlife? Am I afraid nonetheless? Of what? We may be afraid of losing our minds, or our sight, or our ability to move. We may dread incontinence, or the general helplessness and dependency of needing expensive personal care. We may be afraid that we will be in pain, or alone. What other fears do you have? Often, the very act of clearly and honestly acknowledging our fears can help us see ways of beginning to ease them.

At the center of it all is the spell. We, too, may be familiar with a period akin to sleep, or unconsciousness, in our lives. Often, like Sleeping Beauty, we are unaware that we're asleep until we begin to wake up. We might, after several years at a job, gradually—or even suddenly—realize that it is stultifying: we put energy and effort into it, but derive from it no real joy. As we begin to examine our life more closely, we may find that in many ways we have been sleep-walking, doing what is necessary, at home, work, wherever. We have been, maybe, following the dictates of duty, and have lost even an awareness that there *is* no joy. At some point, we may realize that we have let go of life, have lost our true engagement with what gives life meaning, what makes us feel alive. We have been busying ourselves with the demands of tasks—regardless of how much energy they demand—that leave us listless, in a limited life with no sparkle.

Happily, though, the very recognition that we are in such a stultifying situation may indicate that the spell is beginning to wear off. Maybe we can now recognize that what is demanded by duty, relation, even necessity, is not necessarily what gives us freedom or joy. Even if we continue with what we have been doing, we may be able to put it in context, and let go of the view that doing what is necessary is all that is necessary for being alive to life. Perhaps we can be freed from the spell of believing that joy is optional and see that it may be a non-expendable part of our fully-lived life. Maybe, even if we continue with our activities of duty, necessity, and responsibility, we can embrace the freeing demand of opening ourselves to love, and to joy—and become free of the spell. Does it seem too late? Should we just accept that we're old, and that life has nothing left for us? Sleeping Beauty's awakening took a hundred years. Maybe we, at our relatively young age, can look around, and wake up to a life of deeper joy.

CHAPTER 13

The Man, The Horse, The Ox, and The Dog

ANDY

When Zeus made man, he only gave him a short life-span. But man, making use of his intelligence, made a house and lived in it when winter came on. Then, one day, it became fiercely cold; it poured with rain and the horse could no longer endure it. So he galloped up to the man's house and asked if he could take shelter with him. But the man said that he could only shelter there on one condition, and that was that the horse give him a portion of the years of his life. The horse gave him some willingly. A short time later, the ox also appeared. He too could not bear the bad weather any more. The man said the same thing to him, that he wouldn't give him shelter unless the ox gave him a certain number of his own years. The ox gave him some and was allowed to go in. Finally the dog, dying of cold, also appeared, and upon surrendering part of the time he had left to live, was given shelter. Thus it resulted that for that portion of time originally allotted them by Zeus, men are pure and good; when they reach the years gained from the horse, they are glorious and proud; when they reach the years of the ox they are willing to accept discipline; but when they reach the dog years, they become grumbling and irritable.

Ancient Greeks, as indicated in Aesop's fable, believed that Zeus limited human life spans. Born "pure and good," mortals could modify their life expectancies, however, by utilizing their intelligence. (Funerary records and skeletal remains indicate that men in the Classical era died around age forty-four, women nine years earlier.) Zeus also controlled the weather, Aesop informs us. In *The Man, the Horse, the Ox, and the Dog*, a wintry storm creates an opportunity for the protagonist to extend the duration of his life by accepting extra years from three animals who fear that they will freeze to death in the cold.

Aesop's fable rang true to ancient Greeks who doted on babies' innocence and prized the wisdom that accrued with longevity. Nor would it have seemed far-fetched to the storyteller's contemporaries that a horse would ask to share the man's domicile. Horses and humans had symbiotic associations in the classical era. Horses partnered with men in war, races, and hunts; they often conveyed dead mortals to the underworld. Conversely, Greeks centuries ago claimed that people resembled horses. Equine strength (sexual and spiritual) complemented human libido, vigor, intuition, and reason.

Greek mythology personified oxen as kindly, gregarious, peaceful, gentle, and tranquil beasts. Harming or killing oxen, beasts sacred to certain deities, invited divine retaliation. Here, too, there was complementarity. Towards the end of life, elderly Greeks in ancient times hoped to enjoy domestic tranquility and expected care from family and neighbors. Oxen could give them personal traits to adapt to a new stage of life.

Dogs in classical Greek literature were alternately portrayed as friendly or fawning, vicious or docile, gentle or protective. The species were represented in myth as menacing guards of the netherworld. Yet a dog sat by Asclepius, the god of healing. Aesop's characterization of the dog, appropriately enough, had a Janus-faced analog, *The Dog in the Manger*. Dog days disengaged lonely superannuated individuals, but ancient Greeks also were accustomed to interact with elders possessing sunny dispositions. And very old people, perhaps more than the rest of us, harbored thoughts and expressed feelings that, then and now, are hard to predict.

In my opinion, ancient Greeks would not have gasped at the prospect of the fable's protagonist negotiating for extra years from different animals. Scientific evidence in the classical era seemed to validate this presumption. Anaximander of Asia Minor hypothesized that the first humans were born inside fish and reared by sharks. Aristotle's *History of Animals* described man as a "perfect animal" linked biologically to other species.

Aesop could take for granted that his listeners would accept the premise that superior innate intelligence made human life-extension possible. Equine attributes presumably could add to a mortal's glory and pride in the prime of life. The ox offered individuals advancing in age an additional capacity to acquiesce to physical limitations and loss of autonomy. Extra years acquired from a dog might prove a mixed blessing, however. Some very old people grumble; others personify sagacity; still others are irritable and wise, juggling a range of conflicted, deflected, ambivalent moods.

Audiences listening to this Aesop fable probably were left with unanswered questions. How often did animals request shelter in peasants' huts? What body parts or character traits did the horse, ox, and dog offer? Were they in their prime, or had they peaked long before the transaction? Were the extra years a blessing or a curse to the recipient? Did they effect radical, maybe unwelcome, changes in human behavior? What matters—securing greater length of life or enjoying a ripe old age bountifully endowed?

There is good reason for contemporary readers to address any of these questions raised in this fable. Most of us *do* expect to live longer than our grandparents. Men and women spend millions of dollars to replace or tint bad hair, and splurge on cosmetics and remedies promised to reverse other telltale signs of aging. Members of the American Academy of Anti-Aging Medicine have not yet recommended hormonal transplants and testicular implants, as did some prominent North American and Western European scientists, who for centuries have been hawking nostrums. Yet the underlying message of *The Man, the Horse, the Ox, and the Dog*, reverberates in modern times: people want to live long, full of vigor.

The Longevity Revolution has dramatically increased life expectancy at birth and at age sixty-five. Americans born in 1900 on average could expect to live forty-nine years. Now women are more likely than men to anticipate living well past eighty. The number of centenarians has increased fivefold during the past century. Seventy-five percent of this group describe their health to be good or excellent, despite mobility issues and diminished cognitive capacities and sensory impairments. Comparable gains have been registered in Europe, Asia, and countries below the equator.

Current readers and listeners of this fable must interpret Aesop's moral metaphorically, for nowadays it seems to presage a central paradox about growing older. Extra years bring palpable benefits, especially to individuals with financial resources and access to good geriatric care. No longer preoccupied with the busyness of success or raising children, many elders have extra time to engage in new adventures—to tap spiritual resources, to declutter, to cherish relational bonds that really matter.

That said, none of us can deny negative aspects to living extra years, ones that cause pain and suffering in late life. Like it or not, the Longevity Revolution brings to mind the Greek myth of Tithonos.

Eos, Goddess of the Dawn, was so enchanted by her lover's persona and virility that she begged Zeus to grant him eternal life. Alas, she forgot to ask that Tithonos be granted eternal youth as well. The passage of years took its toll. He became a helpless, withered old man and was then turned into a cicada, forsaken by friends and strangers alike.

Similarly, Jonathan Swift in *Gulliver's Travels* satirized the follies of advanced age, which he illustrated during his protagonist's journey to Brobdingnag. There, Gulliver derived distressing impressions of the Struldbrugs—a race of human beasts that aged but never died. The Struldbrugs endured an immortality without the compensatory pleasures and delights that ideally come to mortals in advancing years.

Wisdom, contrary to modern folklore and advice writers, does not always accrue with advancing age. Surviving beyond too many extra years can make even the hardiest of mortals become vulnerable, isolated, and irritable. Anxiety and fear accompany hope and trust in the Longevity Revolution. Sooner rather than later youth fades, and everyone has to deal with physical and mental assaults that accumulate before death. Ageism stings when Millennials taunt elders with social slights ("OK, Boomer"), and when health care professionals demand that older patients "Get out of my emergency room," or GOMERs for short. "Getting old ain't no place for sissies," Bette Davis bluntly declared.

Attaining extra years does not necessarily reduce older people to barking like dogs, however. Technological and pharmacological interventions—as well as medical advances, changing social attitudes, and anti-discriminatory laws—free older persons from being consigned (in most circumstances) to enduring meaningless dog days in a prolonged state of wintry nihilism. We can thrive and flourish in a resilient longevity rarely attained by Aesop's listeners.

CHAPTER 14

Br'er Rabbit and Tar Baby

BARBARA

In order to torment his enemy, Br'er Rabbit, Br'er Fox made a figure out of tar. He put a hat on its head and put this Tar Baby by the side of the road; he hid nearby. Br'er Rabbit came up, saw the Tar Baby, and greeted it: "Good morning. Nice weather," he said. The Tar Baby, of course, said nothing, and Br'er Fox watched.

Br'er Rabbit tried several times to engage the Tar Baby in polite conversation, but the Tar Baby was silent. Br'er Rabbit became frustrated and accused the Tar Baby of being stuck up and rude. Still no response. Br'er Rabbit got increasingly annoyed; he threatened to hit the Tar Baby if he got no response.

Finally he did hit the Tar Baby, and, of course, his fist stuck in the tar; he got more and more frustrated, continued to hit out, and was more and more fully encased in the tar. Now, he became furious that the Tar Baby was holding him down and insisted she let him go. This continued until Br'er Rabbit was completely stuck.

Br'er Fox sauntered out and laughed at his foe. He accused Rabbit of being rude, demanding, and insulting, and said he was going to go out and get some wood; he would then light a fire and barbecue Rabbit. The clever rabbit said that was just fine. Fox could do anything he wanted to Rabbit except throw him in the briar patch, he said, which was his worst fear. It would be fine with Br'er Rabbit to be thrown in a fire, or drowned, or subjected to any other disaster, as long as he wasn't thrown in the briar patch.

Of course Br'er Fox, eager to make the rabbit suffer the most, threw him into the briar patch. There was a lot of rustling noise in the patch, and Fox hung around a bit to see what would happen. After a while he heard something, way up the hill, and saw Rabbit sitting there, comfortably combing tar from his hair. Rabbit yelled down, "Bred and born in a briar patch, Br'er Fox, bred and born in a briar patch!" And he merrily trotted off.

Joel Chandler Harris's *Uncle Remus: His Songs and His Sayings,* published in 1881, was a group of stories told in vernacular from the antebellum slave culture of the southeastern U.S. Harris spent some years on southern plantations, and presented the tales as recountings of stories told in quarters for the enslaved. While some have seen the stories as racist, many have seen them as pointed—but necessarily disguised—anti-racist commentary, shared as a way of bolstering the slaves' sense of community and self-confidence, and suggesting effective ways of maintaining one's dignity and hope despite often brutal and dehumanizing servitude. They address a situation of actual enslavement; but their popularity with people in all life situations speaks to their ability to help us recognize ways in which we are hobbled by less literal kinds of bondage as well.

We have here two opponents in an ongoing war for definitive domination: Br'er Fox and Br'er Rabbit. We begin with Br'er Fox's opening, successful salvo in this story of the war of wits. He presents

Br'er Rabbit with the Tar Baby. Br'er Rabbit finds a supercilious, insulting tormentor who (as Rabbit sees things) goads Rabbit into hitting him, and then continues to ridicule him into what turns out to be a futile effort to teach the Tar Baby a lesson about civility and respect for folks. Of course, when we look at this tarry, provocative creature who harasses Br'er Rabbit into an unwinnable fight, we find nothing of the sort. The insult is nonexistent; the tormentor is not a mean-spirited, clever provocateur, but an inanimate object.

Br'er Fox, unlike the Tar Baby, is a real—and powerful—opponent. His failure here is largely a result of his limited appreciation for Br'er Rabbit's viewpoint. The older we are, the more we can probably, sadly, relate to the fox. How many times have I been "too busy" to appreciate the full complexity of a person standing in front of me? Haven't we all, at some point, seen a boss, or a sales clerk, or a cab driver, or waiter, or someone of a different race or background as nothing more than their function or role? Haven't we done the same thing with coworkers, or even friends? We may look at Br'er Fox and find an uncomfortable similarity with his refusal to see, and treat, Br'er Rabbit as a being equal in worth and complexity. This story may push us to think more deeply about the needs, desires, and gifts that make up the whole person with whom we deal. Br'er Fox was ready to throw Br'er Rabbit into what the fox assumed would be a place of tortuous pain and death. What makes us so easily lose a compassionate humanity and relegate others to a unidimensional cartoon picture? Sometimes, I think, we are drawn to such a viewpoint by our sense of competition, and perhaps an underlying assumption that we need to assert our dominance or superiority in order to "succeed." As we age, less driven by a need to succeed, more accepting of where we are and where others are, we may come to a greater acceptance of the differences and richness of other people's gifts and experiences. We may be able, then, to develop a deeper sense of empathy and understanding, which ends up enriching us.

Unlike Br'er Fox, we can come to see others not just based on what they have to offer us (or how they threaten us), but on who they are and what we might yet learn of the world through them.

We usually think of this story as involving two characters: Br'er Rabbit and Br'er Fox. We tend to see the Tar Baby as ancillary. Probably most of us, at some point, have been seen as ancillary puppets, more or less useful to other people's plans: the "new kid" in the firm, whose allegiance to one partner rather than another, for instance, can help the former move further ahead.

We might have naively assumed, in our first "real" job, that the attention of one of the senior officers or partners was due only to the fact that he recognized our talents more fully than did others. We might have only later—if at all—seen how our good will, effort, and professional gifts were used to his benefit and to the detriment of his peers. While we, too, might have gained from the relationship, it is often the case that our senior's benefit was substantially greater than our own, and that our own may well have come at the price of what could have been meaningful, even useful, relationships developed with our peers. Or we might not have seen the degree to which our eagerness to help the children's soccer team's fund drive was appreciated primarily because it allowed other parents to contribute so little.

Recognizing that others have simply used us to further their own interests is painful because it is essentially dehumanizing to be exploited with little appreciation of our full humanity. How have we responded? Have we been able to see the dismissal of our full selves as a failing on the part of others, or have we felt the demeaning inherent in the situation to be a reflection of own inadequacy? And, on the other hand, have we ourselves, like Br'er Fox, used others as if they were "tar babies," whose only worth lay in their usefulness to us? What do we make of that? Have we changed since then? Do we want to?

In some ways, then, the Tar Baby, far from being ancillary, is the central character: it is only because Br'er Rabbit accorded her the status of a living being that there is a story at all. Br'er Rabbit fights against someone who only has the power he has given her. And it is only at some point between the last, paralyzing head-butt and the beginning of the fox's taunting that the rabbit realizes his own role in this hapless situation. He has allowed Br'er Fox to "get into his head" and immobilize him by using Rabbit's own arrogance and pride in assuming—and confronting—his insult at the tar baby's hands. If the rabbit were not so insistent on needing to be treated with respect, there would be no story. His pride and need for recognition by others make it impossible for him to recognize the truth of the situation. He becomes furious when the Tar Baby won't take off his hat in deference to him. Rabbit's readiness to find insult is his undoing here; it blinds him to the reality of the situation.

One of the most impressive things about the rabbit in this story is the rapidity with which he comes to see his error, and is therefore able to remedy it. Having seen how easily Br'er Fox has duped him into this plight, and how readily he has immobilized himself, he might well fall into the trough of self-abasement and focus on his responsibility for his entrapment. But while he certainly recognizes his role in his own capture, he does not get further embroiled in self-contempt and regret. On the contrary, he seems to grasp the situation, and move rapidly into a problem-solving mode. He seems very clear about his own fault, here, but does not wallow in self-criticism. He moves to positive action.

As we age, and think about our lives, I suspect that most of us can recall situations in which something—our insecurity, fear, arrogance, or some other impediment—led us to misinterpret a situation. We saw an insult when none was intended, or we were unable to look past an insult to the insecurity that lay behind it in the other person. Maybe we tended to bridle when we felt unappreciated, or we withdrew, and felt confirmed in our unworthiness. Or perhaps we were the aggressor, finding fault too often, demanding too much, and lacking compassion out of a sense of smug superiority. Perhaps long-held scars of early pain and suffering, or shields of unacknowledged privilege in our lives, have blinded us to certain realities. Sometimes aging can bring with it a measure of acceptance: of our own limitations, and the limitations of those people and circumstances that have shaped us. We may be able to recognize times when we, like Br'er Rabbit, have seen the world askew, and that misreading has led to the worsening of our situation. As we age, we may be given the gift of clarity and acceptance, of ourselves and others. From time to time, we can then see more clearly, and accept with greater equanimity, the vagaries of life, and the distortions that we ourselves create. Sometimes, in this process of trying to untangle ourselves from the self-inflicted imbroglios, we need help. A push into the briar patch—of therapy, spiritual direction, or personal examination of our roots—may help us comb out the accreted sticky tar of our self-delusion or other paralyzing impediments to the gifts life has to offer.

Rabbit, our hero, is flawed. This is, I think, the central appeal of the Uncle Remus stories: the hero is stubborn, self-satisfied, and frequently stymied by his own flaws. He is a wounded, imperfect hero who nonetheless perseveres—and triumphs. There is hope for all of us equally imperfect folk!

Much behavior based on anger and resentment is ineffectual at best, and often harmful to ourselves, as our story demonstrates. But here, with Br'er Rabbit, we have the added complication of his assessment of the situation having been entirely faulty. All of that painful, enraging sense of mistreatment was in Br'er Rabbit's mind alone. His quickness to feel slighted was itself what trapped him into a state of helpless paralysis.

Such miscalculation, of course, is likely when we have felt

ourselves inadequately appreciated again and again; we assume that to be the case even when it is not objectively so. And often there is a vicious cycle which is created. Feeling disrespected, we react angrily (or coldly, or petulantly), which engenders a lack of respect. We become caught in this as surely as Rabbit was caught in tar. Needing the respect of others in order to respect ourselves is a natural human state; but it may not be a helpful position to be caught in.

The world of paid work is often a hierarchical one, where institutional power looms large, and one may gain respect through position alone, whether or not respect is otherwise warranted. One of the gifts of employment, often, is respect from one's peers and from those one supervises or manages, regardless of the presence or lack of praise from one's own supervisors. In other words, feeling a part of the community of peers can compensate for lack of genuine appreciation from above. It is partly this means of combating feelings of unworthiness and lack of respect that underlies the structure of the Uncle Remus tales. He tells these stories to fellow slaves, especially the youngest and most vulnerable, giving them his attention and respect, while teaching them how to survive—even thrive—in a world in which respect from their "superiors" might never be available. The tale of the Tar Baby can be, in part, a cautionary message about not allowing oneself to be ruled by one's sense of righteous indignation (even if it is, all too often, accurate).

How do we manage when we find ourselves in situations in which we do feel unappreciated or disrespected? In work situations, for instance, where we see others getting raises that we deserve equally but receive inequitably; where those in power verbally or sexually harass us; where we know that our race, age, or gender has unfairly limited our advancement or our participation in higher levels of networking or decision-making; or in public, where something about our physical appearance (skin color, weight, disability, etc.) makes us the object of others' stares, intrusive curiosity, slow service, or outright dismissal? In our family life, when children grow up and are no longer dependent on us, they may (even if temporarily) focus on our perceived inadequacies, robbing us of the pleasure of their admiration. Or our spouse may be so focused on his or her separate life that we feel invisible, unimportant.

We may feel a dismaying sense of loss—loss of power, loss of colleagues, loss of a schedule for our days. Existential questions may begin to loom: What is the point of life? If I am not "contributing" professionally, why should anyone respect me? These same questions become insistent for many of us as we age, regardless of whether or not we retire. Many refuse to do so, anticipating all too well the losses that retirement will entail. But even if we don't retire, as we age, we face increasing evidence of our waning influence: the leaders in our industry become younger and younger, as our own mentors and guides—and then our peers—retire and die, and the new crop of leaders seems to feel perfectly content to do without our (in our view, still relevant and helpful) guidance. Our roles as leaders of professional organizations are taken by younger people, new clients are assigned to younger workers, and our counsel is not requested. It may be that people go out of their way to assure us that we are still important members of the enterprise. But even if it is not hinted that we might be happier without the constraints of work, we realize, if we are willing to face facts, that our input is not so much sought and our presence in the office not so much missed.

It is often the same at home. In fact, the process of becoming irrelevant begins perhaps earlier in the home than at work. Whether we have stayed at home or gone to work, life at home changes as we age. Children grow to adolescence. (What better way to feel disempowered than to face the dismissiveness of a teenager bent on establishing his or her own sense of competence and worth?) They leave home and develop their own lives. And even this is complicated. Many adult children are not setting out on their own but returning to live with their parents. They return as adults with complex views of independence, and family dynamics are often in flux, unclear and confusing.

If we are the stay-at-home spouse of a newly retired worker, the strain of having another adult in the house potentially every moment may not be as blissful as we might once have imagined. For the one who retires, the unscheduled days alone may loom longer and less fulfilling than was anticipated. For those without partners, retirement may deprive us of our main—or only—source of companionship. The roles which sustained us during our earlier adulthood—worker, parent, guide, helpmeet, and sustainer—are no longer required of us, or have changed significantly.

We may become snared in a sense of helplessness, flailing about in a vain effort to locate a source of validation of our worth. We may scurry around, looking for a return of admiration and power. Too often, our fruitless attacks on our situation make things worse, and we are caught in a vicious cycle of increasing powerless frustration. We may feel as helpless and paralyzed as Br'er Rabbit in the embrace of the tar. The shift and challenge is not just internal; it is more than needing to find a new schedule, new companions, worthwhile (or at least enjoyable) ways to spend our time and energy, and more than just a loss of responsibility or energy. It is a loss of our place in the world, a loss of not only our role, but also, often, the respect—and maybe admiration—which we were given in our previous productive life.

So, we can give up, acknowledging that we have been bested, and set our faces toward death. Had Br'er Rabbit chosen that way, he would have looked at himself, covered in tar, and given up. But this well-known tale of the Tar Baby is focused, of course, on Br'er Rabbit's insight, shrewdness, and creativity—outwitting the stronger Br'er Fox's less-clever attempt to ensnare him and kill him.

It has often been noted that those in a group seen as inferior in some way need, in order to survive, to observe and learn about the group in power. In order to protect themselves, they have to know where the specific threats lie. On the most basic level, they need to know the explicit laws the powerful have made, in order to avoid transgressing them. On a more subtle level, the disenfranchised need to know the unwritten rules and expectations, so they do not accidentally offend. More subtly still, they can benefit from figuring out the expectations and desires of those in power—desires of which the powerful themselves may be unaware. The use of this knowledge may result in fawning obsequiousness, or in much more subtle manipulation which results in the subjugated people subverting the power structure to get their desired results. (Those in power have no need for such insightful knowledge of those they dominate, since the explicit and open sources of power lie already in their hands.) In other words, those discriminated against need to learn the expectations and motivations of those in power, while the powerful can—and often do—live in ignorance of the personal and communal desires, motivations, and dreams of the powerless.

The story of the Tar Baby illustrates this dynamic. Although Br'er Fox is tricky, and knows how to play on Br'er Rabbit's resentment of being treated as insignificant, that is the extent of Fox's understanding of Rabbit's motivations. Rabbit, however, well understands Fox's overweening motivation: to kill Rabbit. But Rabbit is aware, too, of Fox's limited understanding of Rabbit's motivation, and that the fox takes the latter's pleas not to be thrown in the briar patch at face value. Fox does not grasp the depth of Rabbit's disinclination to be killed; it doesn't occur to him that Rabbit will do anything—even lie—to avoid dying. And Rabbit is not just determined to stay alive. He is able to stay preternaturally calm enough to think and plan with creativity and cleverness. As a result, Fox is completely outwitted.

Discrimination is a fact of life for aging people in Western culture. The next generation is eager to lead, and therefore eager for us to step aside. What might we learn from Br'er Rabbit? One of his most striking characteristics, it seems to me, is his ability to accept his situation with equanimity, and to calmly and open-mindedly look at options that might lead him to his goal (to stay alive). In order to have a workable plan, he needs to fully understand the motivation and needs of Fox and to take them into account. Fox is angry at Rabbit's arrogance, thinking he's "the boss of everybody." So Rabbit skillfully underscores, through his humility and pleading, that Fox is definitely in charge. He accepts that Br'er Fox's overriding desire is to kill Br'er Rabbit as painfully as possible. So he sets out to convince the fox that what is in fact Rabbit's greatest desire—his only hope, in fact—is his greatest fear. He uses his rhetorical and acting skills to make this point—puts his whole being into his lie—and is fully rewarded. We may not face a situation in which our very existence is at stake (or we might, depending, for example, on how end-of-life care is managed), but we certainly face situations in which, unless we understand our institutional, political, or other adversaries, we will be unable to advocate for ourselves, whether individually or in groups. Merely taking the position that our opponent is wrong (morally, factually, empathetically, etc.) may be ineffective, unless we also take seriously the motivations, strengths, and weaknesses of those whose attitudes and actions we would like to change. We are not necessarily called to duplicity, of course. But safeguarding our own well-being, or very existence, may depend on our being as perspicacious as our friend, the rabbit.

But sometimes we feel discouraged and helpless. Might it be literally a saving grace to be able, when all seems lost, to make an effort to re-conceptualize the situation? Br'er Rabbit refuses to see his predicament in terms of being helplessly dependent on the cruelties of Br'er Fox—although he is. He refuses to cede all the power to the one who seems to have him totally in his power. He thinks outside the box, defining the situation not as one in which he is helpless, but one in which his physical body is powerless while his mind and mouth are not. The briar patch can be seen either as the worst, most dangerous, murderous place, or as the place that will end the pain and helplessness, a place where he could begin anew.

Aging people can fall into assumptions about impending disaster and dissolution. For many, retirement looms like a death: the end of productive life, the death of the useful citizen, the descent into insignificance, mental fogginess, immobility, and despair. We may see the Young Turks replacing us at work as having "won," and we as having lost. If the prize is the running of the corporation, the courtroom, the classroom, the mailroom, or the kitchen, perhaps they have won. If the prize is the best, most sculpted, strongest, fastest, sexiest body, maybe the younger generation beats us. Perhaps we could reimagine our situation, accepting the loss (no doubt the scraping off of all that tar was not much of a joy), but recognizing that there might be a freedom, too. We might have an opportunity to see what we're like when not only the self-importance and sense of hard-earned power and influence, but also the accreted stress and exhaustion of professional struggle is stripped away. We might be able to return to the simpler life in which we were bred and born, before all the mastered abilities and hard-won strengths of adult-hood, and see with new eyes what that essential identity looks like now. Maybe there were gifts that we needed to ignore in order to get where we got, roads not taken that are still navigable. If the goal is not the ruling of the world (or our family life or workplace), then what might it be? Something having to do with using our gifts so far un- or under-used? Something involving what we have learned of the world? Something about the opportunity offered for greater serenity, deeper focus, and a less-frenziedly driven approach to the meaning of life?

Similarly, even as we face the finality of our mortality, Br'er Rabbit's ability to accept the reality of his situation with a measure of equanimity might be of use. He does not give us an example of denial, or some energetic fantasied miracle, but he sees reality clearly and suggests that the briar patch from which we were birthed may still await us. Our end may not be simply the dissolution of self, but some kind of life in whatever place, space, or existence from which we came. We often rail against that final destination, fighting with all our might against what looks to most like nothing more than a place of death and destruction. And yet it is that place of apparent nothingness from which we first were born. Where is it? Is a return to that apparent "nothingness" just that? Or is it a great gift of reunion with our deepest home? Is death the worst thing? If not, might we look serenely toward a time when we are finished here and ready to go back home, with Br'er Rabbit?

CHAPTER 15

The Prodigal Son

BILL

A father has two sons. The younger one asks the father for his inheritance, and the father grants his son's request. The son is wasteful and extravagant, however, and squanders his fortune. Destitute, he returns home and begs his father to accept him back as a servant. To the son's surprise, instead of scorning him, his father welcomes him warmly and throws a party in his honor. Envious, the older son refuses to participate in the festivities. The father, however, tells the older son: "You are ever with me, and all that I have is yours, but your younger brother was lost and now is found."

Back in my ministry days, this was one of those daunting passages that, sooner or later, you had to tackle for the Sunday sermon. Being such an iconic tale, you approached your task with a healthy dose of fear and trembling. What fresh interpretation could you possibly bring to it that your parishioners hadn't heard a dozen times before? What insights could you pull from it that would make them sit up in the pews and take notice, not just of the story itself but—equally crucial—of your own oratorical talents? And where to start, for despite how short it is, there are enormous themes coursing through it—guilt, regret, shame, loss, forgiveness, love—and such larger than life characters as well: the younger son who demands his share of his father's inheritance, blows it on dubious activities in "a far country," and comes crawling back home; the kind-hearted father who greets him at the gate upon his return with open arms and calls for a feast in his honor; and the older son who has kept his nose to the grindstone yet grumbles at the irony of his father effusively forgiving his loser-brother and not once throwing a feast for him.

With lots of life experience now under my belt, I can, of course, see the story through the eyes of each of these players in turn. (Interestingly, no women appear in the cast—no mother or daughter, sister or wife—which suggests that our storyteller, Jesus, might have had a patriarchal bias. But that's a matter to consider at another time.) If I'm honest, though, I've always identified most with the older brother, even if as the baby of a family with two other siblings, both of them sisters, I never had a younger brother to be older than. For better or worse, I was the proverbial "good boy"—didn't smoke, didn't drink, didn't stay out all hours of the night—a behavior that, looking back, I fear was to my detriment developmentally. If I had my life to live over, I'd have done a thing or two differently, have taken more risks, lived more on the wild side. Still, there's often been this strain of martyrdom that underlies my outlook on the world and that links me, psychologically and emotionally, to the older brother—a point that I'll return to later. First, though, let me say a bit about the younger one.

There's something about his part in this story that's always seemed unfair to me. Who does he think he is, asking in advance for his share of his father's inheritance, only to get as far away as he possibly can and squander it on loose living? One can imagine a modern day version, a spoiled brat, bursting with a sense of entitlement, and money, who heads off to Vegas and blows it all on slot machines and poker games. Or off to Wall Street and, selling his soul to the almighty dollar, sinks his savings into some investment scheme that is heralded to yield unheard-of returns, only to have the markets go tumbling overnight. Or, through a series of poor choices, ill-fated escapades, and short-sighted ventures, gets embroiled in the sordid business of alcohol and drug addiction, of using and being used. Or a child prodigy, brimming with promise, who ignores the call to nurture her talents—for singing or writing, for leadership or service, for making the world a better place—and ends up bottoming out in a pit of despair: a failure, a Lost Soul.

There are thousands of them out there, not just on Skid Row or in the back rows of AA meetings, or the back wards of nursing homes or psychiatric units, but everywhere around us and above us, even (sometimes especially) in the halls of power. It's a trajectory that lives can always take, for there are no guarantees. However supportive our parents might have been, however fine a family we may have come from, however privileged our lot starting out, certain less-than-positive traits can emerge as dominant within us, or circumstances can contrive to jade us and pound us down, or a string of unhealthy relationships can sour us on the dream of true romance, leaving us lovelorn and alone.

But then, having reached rock bottom, our hapless hero has a revelation. Recalling how kindly his father was, how indulgent almost, and realizing that he has nothing to lose except his pride (of which there's none left anyway), he resolves to head back home. And his resolution would seem sincere enough, though—who knows?—it could be yet another conniving calculation. Either way, home is bound to have changed. "You can't go home again," says the writer Thomas Wolfe. The farm will have aged, and so will the father, and aged doubly no doubt because of never having heard from his way-ward lad and having assumed therefore that he was dead—such as, sadly, many a parent has experienced, never knowing what became of their child: *ambiguous loss*, psychologists call it. No phone calls, no emails, no postings on Facebook just to say that "I'm okay, I'm alive, don't worry." So, sensing such sadness might be weighing on his father's heart—although, just as likely, wanting to save his own skin—the young man buys a bus ticket home after bumming the fare from some soft-hearted stranger, and—as, in fact, I myself once did. It was for an assignment in seminary that required me to live on the streets of Toronto one weekend in mid-winter and then write a report of my experience. Let me digress for a minute and tell you the story ...

Before setting out on Friday afternoon from my residence on campus, I took care to dress the part—my face left unshaven for a few days prior, my body odor similarly unchecked, a ragged old coat featuring an assortment of unexplained stains, and a pair of scuffed-up work boots, in the toe of one of which I'd stuffed a five dollar bill, just in case. I began my adventure by panhandling my way down to Cabbagetown, as the city's skid row region was referred to at the time. Knowing I was slumming, though, and that it would be over in 48 hours, I found it, all in all, an amusing outing, and an enlightening one as well. One scene that stands out, for instance, is of folks catching sight of me shuffling slowly toward them and then scooting to the other side of the street lest they have to look me in the eye as I hit them up for a handout. That first evening, I remember loitering outside a downtown honky-tonk waiting to intercept its patrons, coming and going and feeling no pain, who were bound to take pity on a ne'er-do-well like me and open up their wallets in response. One seasoned veteran of the streets was keen, however, to include me in his own get-rich-quick caper, which involved performing special favours for said patrons in the men's washroom. As diplomatically as I could, I declined the offer to be mentored in this shadowy means of making ends meet and ambled back to the Salvation Army, where earlier I had left my name on the list so that I could spend that initial night inside. Perched uncertainly on a top bunk in a barren, barracks-like room, with much snoring and coughing around me, it was an edgy ordeal of itching and scratching, due to ticks or lice, I wasn't sure which. And of keeping one eye open lest someone make off with my boots, which I'd taken care to lace together and tuck beneath my pillow but which made for a lumpy night's sleep.

Next morning, crisp and chill, having been booted out of the Sally Ann by 7 a.m., I fell in with a ragtag string of fellow down-and-outers—most of them prodigal sons and daughters in their own right, homeless and adrift—meandering along the twenty-odd blocks toward the Fred Victor Mission for the free lunch that the good people who ran the place provided every day. Following a boring afternoon of aimless roaming, periodically begging a stranger for change, I spent my second night outside, on my own, huddled above a warm air vent behind a building on campus just a few streets over from my dorm—so near and yet so far, a "far country" for sure—my blanket a sorry clumping of cardboard and newspapers that I'd gathered in my travels and had to keep repositioning around me lest I wake up dead.

The following morning found me curled up, not at all comfortably, in a straight-backed plastic chair in the waiting room of a downtown bus station. I was trying to snatch some extra shut-eye between intrusions by the manager bent on shooing away me and my compadres (also sleeping things off) for taking up space intended for bona fide travellers, and for generally lowering the tone of the place. Later, totally playing (and smelling!) the part, I muttered my way through the Sunday morning service in the back pew of a posh downtown church, then crashed the coffee hour afterwards. There, my shabby attire clashed sharply with the tailored suits and mink coats of its well-heeled members. The minister, who was also one of my professors and soon saw through my disguise, was distinctly unamused.

Eventually, after a few more hours of empty-stomached wandering, I made my way back to my room on campus, to the dining hall for supper, and to my status as a student in good standing. The younger brother in our story, though, had no such assurance that his own return would be this positive. Just the opposite. His expectations had sunk about as low as they could go.

So now, then, we turn briefly to the father. I've touched on my own father issues earlier in this book, so there's no need to dredge them back up here. In fact, the father in this story is basically beyond reproach, except that, looking on from the outside, we might be justified in finding him too soft-hearted, a pushover almost. Certainly not the sort of parent with whom, sadly, too many sons and daughters get saddled, who abuse them or abandon them or are otherwise less than parental, and are the last person in the world that they'd want to go home to. In contrast, this chap is a good man. In the eyes of his clean-living, law-abiding neighbors, however, he would have had every right—and perhaps this was part of Jesus' point—to stand on principle. They would have deemed it more dignified, and more godly, to adopt a stern, standoffish attitude towards his good-for-nothing offspring crawling back to him, half-starved (having eaten little more than humble pie), and begging contritely to be treated not as a son, which status he knew that he had forfeited, but as a hired servant.

What does the father do? As soon as he spies his long-lost lad plodding up the lane—perhaps because he, too, had been a prodigal son to his own father, and thus had been there, done that, and gotten the T-shirt—he breaks rank with custom, opts for compassion over common sense, and, as the Good Book puts it, "ran and put his arms around him and kissed him." Not at all what his peers would have expected, nor indeed the son himself, whose prepared speech is waved summarily aside, and he finds himself fitted with the finest robe and thrown a welcome-back gala. "For this son of mine was dead," proclaims the overjoyed dad, "and is alive again; he was lost and is found."

"I once was lost but now am found," writes John Newton in his classic hymn, "Amazing Grace." Lost and found, writes the Canadian literary scholar, Northrop Frye, is "the framework of all literature"; the story of "the loss and regaining of identity." The old, old story, in other words—"the story that's told so often, of how man once lived in a golden age or a garden of Eden or the Hesperides, or a happy island kingdom in the Atlantic, how that world was lost, and how we someday may be able to get it back again"—whether in this life or the next.

My mother has morphed into what I like describing as "a sweet little bundle of love." That said, she's also an addict. She's hooked on hugs, those she receives each day in her interactions with the folks she meets in the facility where she lives—fellow residents, personal support workers, servers in the dining room, staff at the front desk. My father having passed away a few years ago at the age of ninety-eight, she is now of course a widow, but she's fallen in love once again. This time, it's with Kris Kristofferson of country music fame, country music being grounded firm and deep on the solid rock of honky tonks and broken hearts, of cheatin' and drinkin', lyin' and losin', lovin' and leavin'.

In a Nashville church one Sunday morning, the story goes, Kristofferson had a prodigal-son experience of his own that was so overwhelming, it inspired him to write one of his best-known pieces, "Why Me?" "Why me, Lord?" he sings; "What have I ever done / To deserve even one / Of the pleasures I've known?" Each time mother asks Alexa to play it, she is moved to tears—happy tears—because the song reminds her of how thankful she is for her own life, still kicking at one hundred, and for all the love she feels herself encircled by. She surprised me one day, for instance, by telling me that she felt like she was "already halfway in heaven." "Why's that?" I asked cautiously, concerned that she'd had some sort of premonition about her death. "Well," she replied, "it's because I'm surrounded by so many angels."

You might say that she felt she was halfway *home*, as most spiritual traditions propose awaits us, in one form or another, on the other side of death. Witness the lyrics with which many a hymn is laced: "Coming home, coming home, /Never more to roam; /Open wide Thine arms of love, / Lord I'm coming home"; "Home, weary wanderer, home"; "Some glad morning, when this life is o'er, / I'll fly away;/To my home on God's celestial shore." I'll be sneaky here and skirt the whole question of what, or whether, "heaven" is, and how it might be "home," though there's no shortage of near-death-experiencers who insist that it is. The longing for a sense of home, a sense that, somewhere, some when, and despite our several faults, we are accepted just as we are by a presence that loves us unconditionally—illusory or not, this is deep-seated within us and is the sign, some say, of our ultimate destiny and origin as spiritual beings. Certainly, the experience of coming home is so archetypal that it is integral to one of the seven basic narrative patterns that, as I've mentioned before, run through the world of stories everywhere, from the *Odyssey* of Homer to the plot-lines of Hollywood to works of the most sophisticated fiction, namely "Voyage and Return."

The voyages we take in life can assume a multitude of forms, from heading off to university, to taking our lover's hand in marriage, to asking for our share of the family estate and setting forth to see the world. This, however, the older brother doesn't do. Not that he secretly doesn't want to, nor that he isn't involved in any sort of voyage at all. He could be married for all we know, and could have embarked on the humbling journey of being a partner and a parent. Such details we aren't provided in this bare-bones tale. In any case, he doesn't leave home and set out on the journey of life in the grand, dramatic, if ill-fated, manner that his younger sibling does. He doesn't venture far outside his comfort zone, doesn't throw himself into the real world, the cruel world, doesn't face head-on the slings and arrows of outrageous fortune. Basically, and perhaps with good reason, he plays it safe.

This, in fact, was me. As I say, there's a lot of the older brother in me, or at least there was, for (without going into detail) I went on to make up for lost time and enjoy my rightful younger brother days. But for my first thirty-seven years, although I trundled off to university and learned a thing or two there, I soon enough followed in my father's footsteps and became a minister myself. In that role, I did, of course, encounter all kinds of people, more than a few of them lost souls of sorts, at their wit's end, their life's end, the end of their rope. And I remember that afternoon in the Badlands of southern Saskatchewan when I assisted one of them in working through Step Five of the 12-Step Program that he had pledged himself to as a member of AA, requiring that we "admit to God, to ourselves, and to another human being, the exact nature of our wrongs." So, I saw lots of the real world, but it was always a vicarious view and—notwithstanding that one brief weekend on the streets—from a distance. Granted, I crawled as best I could inside of my parishioners' broken hearts and breakdowns, and 24/7, walked with them along their lonesome roads as compassionately as my imagination would allow. But by virtue of my position as a man of the cloth, whom my parishioners, and even myself in a sense, perceived as being above it all in some purer moral realm, I was shielded from such misfortunes myself. Which you'd think would be a good thing, except that, deep down, I felt forever on the outside looking in at Life in all its rawness and reality. Yes, I carried my people's stories in my heart, and sometimes found myself living their lives for them—not unlike the writer, John Steinbeck. In his touching book *Travels with Charley*, he recounts a conversation that he had once with the warden of a park where he and his dog, Charley, were camping for the night. After listening to the man's tale of woe about a less-than-happy marriage, he writes how, as the warden drove off in his truck, "I lived his life for him and it put a mist of despair on me." As for me, I resented being unable to live my own life instead.

I remember Sundays, after hurling everything I had into the sermon—which I'd sweated over all week long and sacrificed my Saturday evening to tweak to a tee—and after shaking hands with parishioners as they scooted off to their happy family dinners, heading back to my apartment (which hardly felt like home), huddling under the covers, and feeling deeply sorry for myself, convinced that Life was, slowly but surely, passing me by. Plus, I knew that my phone could ring at any minute and I'd be summoned to the hospital to comfort some parishioner, or have to listen ad nauseam to some lonely heart at the other end of the line going on and on about how depressed they were, and generally have to be all things—except myself—to all people at all times. On occasion, for example, there might be a lovely and (I'd find out later) available woman sitting in the pew, but my conscience soon assured me that it would be unseemly to ask her out. Unlike Kristofferson, then, there were pleasures I did *not* know and that, for the greater good, I believed I must deny myself. People want their ministers to be married, a senior colleague once advised me, but they don't want them to date. Dating implies uncertainty, tentativeness, and playing around, not the straight and narrow path of fidelity and commitment that's befitting of a man of God. So, however "cool" my parishioners might have thought me—and there were other ways, too, in which I reined in my God-given urges—I lost much of myself in the mix. Which means that since leaving that vocation, after eleven years of giving it my all, I've been on this massive journey to recover myself, or as the case may be, to *dis*-cover myself.

Carol Pearson, in her book *The Hero Within: Six Archetypes We Live By*—which builds on the legacy of Carl Jung and Joseph Campbell, famous for drawing our attention to "the hero's journey"—articulates precisely the inner predicament that I was experiencing prior to setting out on my own journey. "Martyrdom," Pearson writes, "often is used to camouflage cowardice." "Martyrs," she says—the martyr being one of the archetypes that she identifies—"can hide behind this mask of being good and unselfish as a way to avoid taking their journeys, finding out who they are, or taking a stand." Martyrdom, she adds parenthetically, is "a trap for women" in particular, but once again, that's a topic for another reflection.

My journey, though, has by no means been easy, from the time I cashed in my modest pension from the church so that I could finance returning to university (not unlike asking for my share of the family inheritance) to where I am now as a (retired) professor in a field I'd barely even heard of before my forties. This journey, this voyage onto the high seas of ideas, this adventure of following my bliss into a broader realm of service, has surely had its ups and downs. And it has led me down the labyrinthine ways of more conferences and courses, more workshops and travels, more presentations and publications than I can tally up, all dealing with the narrative complexity of human life. This, in short, you could say, has turned out to be my mission.

Yet some would say that the scholarly life is still a comparatively sheltered life, not nearly as hurly-burly as, say, the world of business. Be that as it may, it's been busy enough for me, and has had more than its share of stresses and tensions, diversions and disappointments, dark times and dead ends. Overall, however, it's been a glorious ride, one I wouldn't have missed for all the world. And it's been a wonderful—even providential—fit for my peculiar collection of curiosities and quirks. As far as my life's work is concerned, I've clearly found my niche, my Home, one that has provided mightily in terms of meaning and purpose and fulfilment in life. And I don't feel the least bit burnt out, as I reckon I would have become if I'd remained much longer in ministry, and kept on, martyr-like, older brother-like, attending to everyone else's welfare but my own, my resentment growing more acidic by the day.

That said, I'm finally into full-on retirement, so like many in this position, I'm concerned about what comes next, how I'll put in my time after stepping off the academic ladder. I'm not *that* concerned, admittedly, since as long as my eyesight holds out I can keep on writing, and the added time to do so will be welcomed indeed. But not many have this avenue in front of them, and a comparatively inexpensive one at that, as an ongoing source of meaning and purpose in life. For lots, alas, the Third Age can be a lost age.

There can be a lostness about later life that is unsettling, to say the least. As there can be, no question, about midlife as well. Witness Dante's description in this famous passage from *The Inferno*: "In the middle of the journey of our life,/ I came to myself, in a dark wood, / Where the direct way was lost." But later life can be particularly disorienting, and perhaps especially so for men, whose sense of identity can too often be tied up with their profession, their job. *Who am I, and what am to do, to be, now that I'm no longer a professor, a minister, a doctor, whatever?* One writer calls this a crisis of meaning. A close colleague of mine, also retired, teetered recently on the brink of a serious depression, in which his anxiety around the meaning of retirement for him personally, I reckoned, played no small role. Psychologist Erik Erikson states the issue starkly concerning the "crisis" we face in the final decades of life, where our options are, on the one hand, *ego integrity*, which I take to mean, basically, "pulling ourselves together": a process which Florida Scott-Maxwell describes as "possess[ing] all you have been and done" and becoming "fierce with reality." On the other hand, there is *despair*.

Of course, it's never just one or another. It's not that neat. Whatever feeling of integration we might attain can still have—maybe *needs* to have—a strand or two of despair running through it, to temper it, ground it, render us that much fiercer with reality. Yet there is nothing harder to encounter, especially when it emanates from someone close to the end of their days, than the nagging, grinding experience of despair that comes from a life not well lived, a life riddled with regret over lost opportunities and wasted years, a life that they are living alone, in an institution maybe, because their loved ones have moved away or passed away and there is no one left who knows their story or, more important, cares. Arthur Kleinman, one of the early figures in "narrative medicine," captures the matter with great poignancy when he writes that "few of the tragedies at life's end are as rending to the clinician as that of the frail elderly patient who has no one to tell their life story to." We might call this special brand of lostness *narrative* lostness. If so, the remedy I recommend is narrative *care*.

Narrative care means listening closely and respectfully, openly and compassionately, for a person's unique story, in all its complexity and mystery, layeredness and depth, with its highs and its lows, its learnings and losses, its disappointments and regrets. I'm referring, for each of us, to the story of our own little journey through the world, the journey of our own unique life, a life that no one else but us could have lived. I mean the story by which we understand who we are, the story that, at base, is inseparable from our emotions, our relationships, our values and beliefs, our identity, our whole way of being in the world. Having this story listened to and validated can help us expand it and explore it, and ferret out its Truth, in the process returning us to ourselves, our "*true* selves" perhaps. I call this the autobiographical adventure, an adventure that leads beyond ourselves, sooner or later, into that common, human region where we see that we *all* have stories. And in those stories lies a cache of wisdom from which, if we would but stop and listen, we all could gain so much.

Before I get carried away with happy endings, though, and start going on about age itself as a massive adventure, let me wrap up my ramblings on a more somber note. For what we have here is a parable that we can read ourselves into not just as individuals but in broader terms as well.

As I write this, entire countries have been under lockdown off and on because of a virus that has largely outwitted science. The situation invites hyperbolic comparisons. We, the human race, are the prodigal son on a planetary scale. We have squandered our inheritance of intelligence and imagination, and abandoned our calling as carers of each other and stewards of the earth. Thus, far from greeting us at the gates with open arms and shunting our apologies aside, Mother Nature is paying us back for our wastefulness and willfulness, our centuries of raping the environment and soiling our nest. And, with climate change and all the upheaval that goes along with it, she is doing so with a determination we seem powerless to stop.

Is all of this just a blip on the screen, from which the markets will eventually bounce back to business as usual? A minor reality check, a pressing of the "reset" button, after which we pick up where we left off? Or are we on the edge of a whole new normal, in a far country such as we've never before known, with no clear path back home? As with other stories featured in this book, we find ourselves not outside this story looking in, but inside it looking out. We are squarely in the middle of the plot, with no guarantee of the happy-ever-after ending that the younger son was shown.

Or, at least, that's one way of interpreting the matter. There are other ways, no doubt. Which is where you, dear reader, enter in ...

CHAPTER 16

Jam Yesterday, Jam Tomorrow, But Never Jam Today

BARBARA

[Alice said to the Queen,] "But really you should have a lady's-maid!"

"I'm sure I'll take you with pleasure!" the Queen said. "Two-pence a week, and jam every other day."

Alice couldn't help laughing, as she said, "I don't want you to hire me—and I don't care for jam."

"It's very good jam," said the Queen.

"Well, I don't want any today, at any rate."

"You couldn't have it if you did want it," the Queen said. "The rule is, jam tomorrow and jam yesterday—but never jam today."

"It must come sometimes to 'jam today,'" Alice objected.

"No, it can't," said the Queen. "It's jam every other day: today isn't any other day, you know."

"I don't understand you," said Alice. "It's dreadfully confusing!"

"Jam yesterday, and jam tomorrow, but never jam today." At first, this seems not so bad. Every other day there is jam; and possibly jam—hardly nutrient-rich—isn't really necessary more than three or four mornings a week. But the Queen makes the reality of the situation clear very quickly, and we can see this rule as both arbitrary and gratuitously punitive. Why mention jam at all if it is never to be had? Why dangle it in front of one, as an almost-obtainable treat? Fortunately, Alice "doesn't care for" jam, so the rule is a theoretical deprivation. Nonetheless, it seems a bit cruel to brandish it, offering the never-to-be-had jam as a job inducement. There are aspects of our culture, though, which seem to present us with this very situation.

JAM YESTERDAY

Yesterday we had jam. Wonderful, delicious jam. The time we won the state championship. The time we got one hundred per cent on that math test. The time the whole family went apple-picking on the most perfect fall day, and all contentedly munched on those just-tart-enough fruits during the drive back home. (Before the fight over the unfinished homework—let's not dwell on that part of the day.) First love. The interview that went so well; we knew before the call came that we had the job. Second love. The perfect wedding. The promotion that *did* come, finally, after that disastrous second year. The baby's first laugh. Her graduation from college, and first job. That huge contract we got—or the case we won, or the book we sold, or…. We have those memories, and can bask in the sweetness of jam-filled joys long past.

Of course, that jam is temporary. All we have, after we've tasted it, is the memory. We know what jam tastes like, but we are not having any today. And so the jam of yesterday is bittersweet. It is connected to a sense of loss—all those things we once had but have no longer. As we age, that list grows longer: parents, friends, jobs, impressive athletic skills, the ability to have a couple of drinks and have fun rather than immediately fall asleep, the belief that tomorrow will dawn more brightly, and that great things are within our reach, that our best years are ahead of us. There are great gifts which we have lost forever: a specific relationship that can never be replicated, for example. Part of the mourning process often involves a re-evaluation of that relationship, and we may face more clearly some of its limitations: the way in which our father treated his home as a castle and didn't really take others' feelings into consideration when they conflicted with his own needs; our sister's criticisms, which bespoke, as we now see more clearly, an enduring competition that made visits uncomfortable after a day or so; our best friend's inattention to the calendar or clock, and the times spent wondering if he would arrive at the chosen place or not. The memory, and the ways in which that love changed us, are not lost, and although they are not always glowing, they have formed us, and are often sustaining as time goes on. After loved ones' deaths, we relive the deep warmth, the times of joy, the shared sense of humor, the genuine love between us. We also recall the pain and disappointment of the relationship. But we may see, too, the ways in which it made us stronger, showed us possibilities we might otherwise not have seen. We might be able to celebrate the empathy and concern for those in trouble that was born from our own losses. But that jam, of these particular loves, will never be served again, and the promise of "jam tomorrow" does not assuage the loss of that lovely, sweet, tangy—even sometimes over-tart—taste of love lost to death.

There are other losses of sweetness which we grieve, of many kinds: lost jobs, financial setbacks, grievous losses resulting from hurricanes or other disasters; losses of physical health or strength as a result of accident or age or disease; loss of sustaining hope; and many others. Some—perhaps an uncomfortably many—are losses due to our own faults, mistakes, cowardice, highhandedness, over-confidence, ineptitude, lassitude, or cruelty. We grieve, often while retaining those flaws. In many cases, whether we are implicated in the grief or entirely innocent, we know that what we have lost will not be reinstated. It is a jam of yesterday that will not reappear tomorrow.

And the Queen may bring to mind another type of loss as well, that of missed opportunities: the jam we were served but didn't bother to put on our toast. We assumed it would always be there: the weekend in Chicago which we refused because the one who offered it seemed a bit dull and maybe slightly full of himself, but mainly because he seemed bland in comparison with the live-wire we had just met—who burned out within a couple of weeks, after Chicago was lost forever. Or that early job that we felt was so far beneath our abilities that we couldn't be bothered doing all the scut work it required, but which, we found out after we had left it with less than a sterling recommendation, could have led to something much more interesting and challenging, had we only demonstrated our willingness to do what was asked in a thorough, professional way. Or the trip to Santa Fe right after college with a bunch of classmates who were all going in different directions and wanted a last time together; you felt you needed to get straight to work and didn't have time to waste on a holiday when a career needed to get started—and now Santa Fe isn't Santa Fe and you've lost touch with the friends, some of whom are still friends with each other because they valued those relationships and worked to sustain them. It is not just that the jam is gone. It is often that we never fully appreciated it when we had it.

JAM TOMORROW

"Jam tomorrow" is the rallying cry for parents, teachers, religious leaders, and so many others in our culture who have responsibility for the shaping of young minds. Most of us have been bludgeoned for decades with the cudgel of self-denial for the sake of future gain. We are to study hard now so that we'll get a good job later, or we need to suffer through punishing, seemingly endless athletic practices and games so that we might have the pleasure of beating others once we have mastered the sport. We are taught to cede to others the advantage we might take, or the fun we might have, in the hopes of, in the end, being the recipient of those privileges and more as we rise in life. Instead of buying what the advertisers are so eager to make us want, we are told to save our money so that it will grow into a fortune able to provide whatever we want later; skip the night on the town to stay on at the office so that promotions and raises will allow us to do and buy whatever we want later; put off having children until we are in a position to "comfortably" raise them. In short, forgo the jam today so that we will have plenty of jam tomorrow.

There is a great temptation to take this as a moral, rather than a practical, edict. We may see those who deprive themselves as morally superior to those who don't, even when their self-deprivation is a calculated procedure whose aim is simply to increase the reward later on. In our highly capitalistic society, where those with money tend to be seen as superior to those without, this superiority is likely to take on moral overtones, and those who "indulge" themselves, even when at no cost to their wealthier neighbors, are seen as morally deficient. Enjoyment itself takes on negative ethical overtones. We may even come to see those who have little as being responsible for their poverty. Clearly, we may think, they didn't focus on the appropriate hard work to get to a more impressive state in life. If they had done the right thing, sacrificed appropriately, they would be doing well now.

Even when we do not judge others for what we assume to be their inadequate self-denial, we ourselves may suffer from an overabundance of "discipline." Learning from an early age to defer gratification—especially when that deferment is experienced as a permanent denial—may stunt our ability to actually enjoy life's pleasures. All too often, the habit of self-denial can render us unable to delight in those things that we've been saving up for. We no longer really want even the sporty little medium-priced car, never mind the Ferrari that we'd fantasized about; we are so used to spending "free" time on work that we have no real idea of how to spend "unprofitable" time; we have put off having children until our fertility is diminished, along with the energy needed to raise them. It is not uncommon for people to reach professional positions that would, years earlier, have seemed the pinnacle of success. Now they seem mere stepping stones to something greater. They are not the jam we had envisioned, but merely more raw sugar needing to be boiled for future enjoyment. Many of us find the prospect of retirement terrifying, partly because we have lost the knack of enjoying ourselves without a clear "profitable" plan to follow, or a series of well-worn steps leading to future "success" or "career advancement."

Of course, many will argue that a hedonistic approach to life is, if less grueling, much more dangerous. If we do not put off until tomorrow the fun in life, we will never get a job, and certainly never keep one or succeed at it. Every pleasure comes at a price; the jam is not free, and if all we eat is jam, the protein necessary to sustain life will be absent. It is certainly true that if one parties all night, one is unlikely to be able to function productively the next day. But it is also true that Jack can become quite the dull (and depressed) boy if he has no play.

As we age, the promise of jam tomorrow may seem sadly ironic. We become uncomfortably aware that there are increasingly few tomorrows for us, and the jam we can realistically imagine being served is much less rich in diversity than it once was. Where at one time we imagined a near infinitude of sweet combinations of diverse fruits, now it is hard to think of any realistic jam other than strawberry or blueberry: pedestrian flavors, often saccharine, and certainly unimaginative. We've had all the jam we can imagine, and what's left for tomorrow looks likely to be bland institutional imitation of the wild variety we used to have—or at least used to imagine we would have someday. As we age, our world tends to become smaller: what we someday wished we could do has become either unattainable or passé. We've either had it already or never will have it. Physical limitations due to age or ill health may constrain; financial restrictions may curb travel, housing, or entertainment possibilities. We no longer have the luxury of being able to dream great dreams and think that they are pictures of a real future. The limitations of reality intrude powerfully on our visions of endless luscious jams in the future.

But there is another way that aging can shift our understanding of the jam of tomorrow. As we come closer to the inevitability of death, many of us see the end of life as an entrance into another realm, in which the jam is more delectable than we can imagine, and constantly available. Many of us believe in some sort of life after death, and see it as the fulfillment of our greatest desires. As we age, death becomes not an abstract, far-off concept, but an increasingly vivid nearby reality. While few people seek it, and many fear it on a potent visceral level, aging affords us the opportunity to examine our beliefs about this inevitability. Will death be the end? Will it be unending torment? Or will it, as the Queen promises us, be full of jam? If we believe that we will, in some form, exist beyond our mortal death, we may see ways in which we might prepare for that new life: ways in which we may be loving, or generous, maybe to "earn" eternal life, or maybe to experience the joy of generosity while we are still here. Our view of the possibility of a future existence may influence every aspect of our later years.

NEVER JAM TODAY

Having vicariously enjoyed the jam of yesterday and tomorrow, though, we eventually need to return to the jam-free present. The losses, ailments, and limitations of aging are well-known—especially to those doing the aging. Even if we go to the gym every day, eat well, and are generally healthy, there is a gradual slowing. And illness, disease, or accident will eventually take a toll on every one of us. The future is not limitless, and it becomes evident even to the most willfully blind that some hopes will never be fulfilled.

If we no longer can dream of becoming world-renowned in our field, or fabulously wealthy, or twenty-five and gorgeous, or the center of a star-studded social life, or brilliant, or having a perfect family filled with such people, or if we have had such dreams fulfilled and found them to be less satisfying than we assumed they would be; if we are still waiting for the jams of such dreams, maybe we can now let them go, relieved of the pressure they have put on us for so long. The loss of long-held dreams may be painful, even if the dreams were always preposterous. But that loss may free us to enjoy a rich life even without jam. What we may find is the possibility of dreaming different dreams. Maybe it can be freeing to accept the realistic limitations of a truncated future. Maybe we can more deeply appreciate the taste of a lovely ripe apple. Maybe our focus on that unattainable jam has blinded us to an appreciation of what we already have, which may not be the idealized jam, but it may be surprisingly fulfilling. Of course, today is the yesterday of tomorrow. Will we, in whatever tomorrows come our way, be able to remember today as a day well spent, alive in the possibilities that only today can bring? Or will we remember today as the time in which we agonized over the past, and worried about tomorrow?

CHAPTER 17

What the Old Man Does is Always Right

ANDY

An old man sets out for town, after he and his wife decide to sell their horse to obtain food. Having made no sales at the market, the farmer starts to return home. Along the way, he encounters a peasant with whom the old man, who always does what is right, trades his horse for a cow. In the course of the next few hours, the protagonist subsequently trades the cow for a pig, the pig for a goat, the goat for a sheep, the sheep for a goose, and the goose for a hen. When he exchanges the hen for a bag of rotten apples, the old farmer thinks he got the better end of this deal, too. Onlookers think otherwise. A neighbor notes that each transaction was worse than the last; two Englishmen bet that his homecoming will be grim. No worries: what the old man does is always right. His wife, who thinks that all of the transactions were for the best, kisses her husband. In disbelief of the denouement, the English-men give the couple a sack full of gold in return for the bag of rotten apples.

*W*hat the Old Man Does is Always Right is a saccharine fable. It is hard for me to take seriously Hans Christian Andersen's story about a sweetly doting married couple who thank God for letting them see the sunny side of life. Not only do I fully understand the neighbor's relief that he would not have to share the day's events with his own wife, but I would gladly have chipped in to the Englishmen's wager. Incredibly, Andersen's plotline casts the neighbor and the merchants in the wrong. The wife's loyalty and equanimity defy anybody's expectations, even mine as a seven-year-old hoping for sweet dreams as I crawled into bed.

I cannot imagine that my mother ever shared this tale with me, although she reckoned that reading *What the Old Man Does is Always Right* would lull my two younger brothers to sleep. My siblings were three and five by the time she had probably figured out that her firstborn could not be so easily duped. Mom knew something else about me: blessed with big ears, I was able to hear my parents fight in private. Many times, when I watched them open their bedroom door, they acted as if no ill words had been exchanged. Given the dynamics of my family of origin, I certainly deserved to be chastised for eavesdropping.

But someone in the fable has to shout out. This is why Hans Christian Andersen inserted the neighbor and the English merchants into *What the Old Man Does is Always Right*. Who would not be appalled by the farmer's stupid trades? Is the wife really so unconditionally loving to permit Andersen to deliver such a sappy ending? Frankly, I am surprised that the fabulist did not introduce youngsters into the narrative. Wouldn't little kids, overhearing the old man's negotiations, be skeptical about the rectitude of patriarchal wisdom? Wouldn't brats roll their eyes upon being told that this is what happy marriages entail?

Perhaps I give myself and other Baby Boomer children too much credit. Would we have dared to risk speaking truth to power in the

1950s? We were raised in decades that brought prosperity to many adults, whose paths to upward mobility were quite similar. Having struggled through a Great Depression and survived World War II, my parents and their peers found respectable and remunerative professional niches. Thirty-something moms and dads (mine and others I knew, at least) engaged in social lives that mirrored their relentless motivation to attain security and to secure status markers of success unimaginable to their grandparents.

I overheard many of them idly chatting while lounging in country clubs. During office breaks (I suspect), white-collar workers in that Greatest Generation would brag about their children's early accomplishments—Nathaniel was admitted to an Ivy League university, and Sally earned more as an intern than her old man got for his starting salary. My parents and their friends (who, fast forward, were ripening in the prime of life) had every right to savor the fruits of their children's coming of age. After all, they had sowed the seeds on their watch.

Was this not simply the way in which generations succeed one another? Why shouldn't parents rightly enjoy leaving a bountiful legacy? Did they not deserve much credit for making it possible? Conversely, silence reigned (I noticed) when mothers and fathers could not boast and did not swagger. Few of the parents that I knew while I was growing up ever admitted how vicariously they had invested in their children's future success. The proof was in the pudding, as Mom liked to say: parents always did right to shower offspring materially and often emotionally. It compensated, she felt, for deprivations that they had had to suffer as children in the 1930s and 1940s.

My parents, who belonged to the Greatest Generation, were hardly unique in trying to do whatever they thought was right. They delayed gratifying their own desires and needs in order to make decisions patently in their offspring's best interests. They bought homes in neighborhoods with excellent schools. When they were not coaches or chauffeurs, Baby Boomer parents enthusiastically served as den mothers and scout masters.

Now having become a parent myself, I have learned that what the old man does is *not* always right. I wonder whether my parents and their friends regretted their decisions or questioned their options—although, as I said, I never heard adults in the Greatest Generation share doubts or acknowledge reservations about how they went about the business of raising their children. Instead, they took experts' advice, which (to them) verged on gospel truth.

Best-selling authors, with credentials widely advertised by publicists, repudiated mainstream codes of propriety. Disdainfully mocking early 20th-century middle-class virtuosity, experts instructed parents in postwar America to nurture their sons and daughters permissively. In *The Common Sense Book of Baby and Child Care*, Dr. Benjamin Spock assured first-time mothers that they knew more about raising children than they thought. Be flexible, affectionate, and indulgent, the good doctor advised.

English pediatrician and psychoanalyst Donald Winnicott, who was less known in the U.S. than Dr. Spock, delivered an equally supportive and uplifting message. Dr. Winnicott sought to allay anxieties by asserting that it took time to become a "good enough" parent. Much depended, he claimed, on exercising self-care while fulfilling various childrearing responsibilities. Mothers (who were Spock and Winnicott's prime readers) did not have to be "perfect" as long as they tolerated their mixed feelings and hesitant actions in a loving light.

All this guidance, of course, went far beyond my comprehension as a child. Instead, television shows taught me at age ten most of what I knew about parenting. In front of the black-and-white screen, I identified with kids roughly my age—Theodore (a.k.a. Beaver) Cleaver and his older brother, Wallace (a.k.a. Wally). Along with their parents, Ward and June, they starred in *Leave it to Beaver*, a situation comedy that ran between 1957 and 1963. The *dramatis personae* acted out weekly plots in a comfortable setting. They cheerfully mouthed innocuous dialogues, which meshed with my own growing-up experiences. Like Wally and Beaver's, mine was a close-knit family that avoided drama scenes—sometimes because good-enough parents and kids withheld inconvenient truths.

Ward Cleaver looked and behaved like my dad—though I was aware of class differences in their respective upbringings. Television character Ward was a farmer's son who had gone to prep school; competitive scholarships and the GI bill enabled my father, a city boy, to become a corporate executive. Both men were successful professionals, who rewarded their sons' proper behavior—without going overboard. Ward and Dad spared the rod, unless their wives insisted on punishment. And that dreaded sequence of events occurred only if and when mothers thought their reprimands (delivered before the men returned home from work) proved ineffectual.

Even then, the two fathers couched verbal rebukes in aphorisms and allusions. It never occurred to me how generous it was that Ward and Dad listened to their children's versions of what they had done wrong enough to spark their mothers' ire. Contretemps usually were resolved with formulaic promises to do better next time. These fathers may not always have done what was right in this tack, but I definitely must salute them for trying their best.

My mom resembled June Cleaver—though I never saw her vacuum floors dressed in pearls. Nor did my parents sleep in twin beds. Both women comported themselves with dignified calm; they epitomized maternal propriety even during moments of domestic tumult. Ceaselessly cooking and keeping things orderly, neither housewife smothered her boys. Like their husbands, June and Mom encouraged their sons to think for themselves. Occasionally they managed to defuse tensions by permitting the kids to laugh over parental gaffes.

I looked up to clean-cut, straight-arrow Wally. Pitying his awkward forays into adolescence, I nonetheless admired his achievements, so modestly and effortlessly executed. Wally rightly took it for granted that he was destined to attend a good college. Beaver resembled my younger brothers—all of whom (I jealously thought) benefited from benign neglect. Unlike me, the gifted one being primed and disciplined for success, my parents appeared to delight in my siblings' mischievous behavior. I never got away with using their gee-whiz slang and expletives. Wally and Beaver had friends (like ours down the street) who were portrayed as somewhat flawed. One kid was husky, others were ugly and ordinary. And every neighborhood had an Eddie Haskell who got out of trouble with a winningly unctuous smile.

I do not recall many Black or Spanish-speaking characters on *Leave it to Beaver*. None lived near me, either. There were no depictions of rapes, break-ins, or arrests, but all was not utterly beatific in these hometowns. One stay-at-home TV mother basically struggled as a single parent, because her husband was frequently away on long business trips. Divorce (among couples other than Ward and June) was mentioned in several episodes. Nor did the producers shy away from exposing the abuses of alcoholism. None of this was unfamiliar territory to me.

Slightly less credible to my jejune mind was *Father Knows Best*, an Emmy-winning TV show that ran from 1954 to 1960. The series, like *Leave it to Beaver*, extolled warmth, decency, and family love. Jim and Margaret Anderson, who were raising two girls and a boy, assumed gender roles that now seem stereotypical. "Father" was a well-off insurance agent, who was invariably doing something right. Mrs. Anderson played the part of a stay-at-home mom perfectly. Unlike Mrs. Cleaver, Margaret sometimes acted helpless, notably when her female wiles did not work. The children—Betty, Bud, and Kitty—seemed plastic. Life lessons were quotidian—no teenage pregnancies or dropouts made the screen on this series.

When I became a parent twenty years later, I emulated neither Ward nor Jim. Instead, I compared my style of nurturing with my father's. Dad was a good man, who died before my first child was born. What he did was not always right, but Pops cannot be faulted for his role-modeling. I tried to replicate his strengths as I went on to make mistakes of my own doing.

My first wife, Mary, and I duly read bestsellers by Spock and the next wave of professionals; our circle of friends discussed Winnicott's theories with us. But Mary and I adopted a different approach to childrearing. We relied primarily on common sense in raising Emily and Laura. I was a good-enough father, though in retrospect, too often preoccupied with publishing scholarly papers or seeking ways to supplement a decent salary. Mary was a terrific parent. Often having to act as the bad cop, she ably counterbalanced my admittedly lax sense of discipline. Emily and Laura grew up in a progressive university community. Their classmates replicated rites of collegiate passage, indulging in casual sex, selling drugs, and driving cars that their teachers could barely afford.

Mary and I divorced after our kids were raised. We tried to spare Emily and Laura pain, but in the ordeal, one was bruised and the other traumatized. Our now forty-something daughters have strikingly different personalities, yet both are respected for their self-reliance, tenacity, and generosity. Mary and I were lucky raising children—more fortunate than many Baby Boomer parents, whose children ran away, died of overdoses, or committed suicide.

Like the Cleavers, who presumably enjoyed happy lives after the series ended, we managed to avoid tragedy, despite inevitable bumps along the way. The Anderson-family actors' legacy was not so happy in real life. Robert Young, who played Jim in *Father Knows Best*, suffered from depression and alcoholism. Lauren Chapin, who portrayed younger daughter Kitty, was typecast for the rest of her career; sexually abused, she became a drug addict. Buddy, the actor Billy Gray, later revealed to radio listeners the extent to which "a stupid bunch of kids" spewed off-the-screen sarcasm. Only Jane Wyatt, who went from being Mrs. Anderson to play Amanda Grayson (the human mother of another Spock on the science-fiction TV series *Star Trek)*, enjoyed relative good health until she died in her nineties.

Life unfolds in surprising ways: I remarried at sixty-seven, semi-retired at seventy, and now live a contented life. Of particular joy are my two grandchildren, Tabitha, now ten, and Luke, aged eight. They adore my second wife; for some reason, they think that I am a clown. Although Oma and Pop-Pop live six states and a thousand miles away, we get to see each other twice a year. Skype brings us closer. The grandkids tell Oma secrets. I have played virtually no role in raising my grandkids. To my credit, I have wisely resisted the temptation to coach their parents.

Happily, my grandchildren are being raised by mature adults, whom I doubt pay attention to Doctors Spock and Winnicott, much less Dr. Phil. Their dad is humble enough to know that the old man is not always right; Erik plays with the kids every night, delightedly listening to their tall tales and earnest concerns. Emily successfully re-entered a tough job market—after deciding to stay at home until Luke entered kindergarten. Erik and Emily insist that their children figure out for themselves how to resolve spats.

The way Mary and I parented was a far cry from Hans Christian Andersen's sappy fable, and, admittedly, parenting as such is not what it's about. That said, I hope that Erik and Emily never read *What the Old Man Does is Always Right* to their kids. Pop-Pop and Oma watch from afar, taking comfort as the next generation knits together family bonds. We wish them Godspeed and much love.

CHAPTER 18

The Lion, The Witch, and The Wardrobe

BILL

"This must be a simply enormous wardrobe!" thought Lucy, going still further in and pushing the soft folds of the coats aside to make room for her. Then she noticed that there was something crunching under her feet. "I wonder, is that more mothballs?" she thought, stooping down to feel it with her hand. But instead of feeling the hard, smooth wood of the floor of the wardrobe, she felt something soft and powdery and extremely cold. "This is very queer," she said, and went on a step or two further.

A long with her older sister, Susan, and two older brothers, Peter and Edmund, little Lucy has been sent away from London to the rambling country home of a retired professor to escape the horrors of war on the eve of the Battle of Britain. The first day after their arrival being a rainy one, the four set forth on a room-by-room inspection of their digs. Dawdling behind the others, Lucy is drawn to one room in particular, "quite empty except for one big wardrobe; the sort that has a looking-glass in the door." Cautious but curious, she pulls the door open, makes her way in, and emerges, Alice-like, into "the middle of a wood at night-time with snow under her feet and snowflakes falling through the air." The wood is part of Narnia, a wonderland of witches and fauns, magic spells and talking lions, and all manner of features and creatures that make it quite unlike the land that Lucy left behind, however much, in an oddly English way, it mirrors it, too—a parallel universe of sorts.

On more than one front, I've been a late bloomer. As to which fronts in particular, there's no need to go into them here. But one of them, for certain, is being in my mid-twenties and halfway through divinity school before first encountering the book in which this little scene appears, plus other books like it, which, though composed far more recently than those of Andersen or Aesop, were intended, I assume, for far younger readers than me. I can still recall gorging myself night after night on Tolkein's *Lord of the Rings*, stealing time from tomes by the likes of Paul Tillich and Karl Barth that I ought to have been religiously ingesting instead. I found myself getting lost in the epic adventures of Frodo Baggins and faithful pal, Sam Gamgee. And in a lighter though no less engaging way, I got swept up in the adventures of little Lucy and her siblings in the land of Narnia.

One of Tolkien's own pals was Clive Staples Lewis, or C. S. Lewis, as he's best known (or "Jack" as he himself preferred to be called), author of the acclaimed series, *The Chronicles of Narnia*, in the very first volume of which, *The Lion, The Witch, and The Wardrobe*, Lucy's remarkable discovery occurs. From the 1920s through the 1950s, the two were colleagues at Oxford, where Tolkien eventually became Professor of Anglo-Saxon, and Lewis a Fellow and Tutor at Magdalen College. (He was later elected Professor of Medieval and Renaissance English at "that other place," Cambridge.) Along with a coterie of like-minded scholars who called themselves The Inklings, they met weekday evenings at The Eagle and The Child, a local Oxford pub (known affectionately as The Bird and the Baby), for spirited debate on all manner of matters—philosophy, theology, literature, ethics, you name it. Over beer and cider and with a haze of smoke from their cigarettes and pipes swirling around their heads, they would also read aloud to one another excerpts from whatever manuscripts they were writing at the time. About the time that Tolkien was readying *Lord of the Rings* for publication, Lewis began working on *Narnia*.

Some years earlier, I'd read several of Lewis's more stridently apologetic books, like *Mere Christianity* and *The Problem of Pain*, not to mention his imaginative, amusing, and (I felt) ever-so perceptive *Screwtape Letters* and *The Great Divorce*. Unofficially, these works were required reading within the Harvard-Radcliffe Christian Fellowship that I belonged to for two tumultuous years (a whole story of its own!). His unique blend of insight and wit, and his frank, bright prose, grounded me and inspired me. I can easily say that, until my early thirties when I stumbled onto more contemplative writers such as Henri Nouwen, Thomas Merton, Adrian Van Kaam, and eventually Teilhard de Chardin (all of them Roman Catholic, it's worth noting), Lewis had the most profound influence on me of any of the finely-tuned minds that I was exposed to during my seminary training. For better or worse, his writing made a disproportionate impression on my formation not just as a thinker and believer, but as a reader and even writer, too. Quite apart from his conservative theological vision—more a medieval vision, really, even downright reactionary—which made him the darling of the evangelical student set, on North American campuses in particular, his command of the English language in capturing complex insights shaped my spiritual development more tangibly than Niebuhr or Moltmann or any of the others whose arguments I struggled to decipher. And it certainly had a greater impact than anything that my father said as well. Nonetheless, the view of the world that Lewis managed to convey to me by means of it resonated nicely with the more narrow worldview on which the latter had brought me up. At the same time, it challenged and stretched that worldview, infusing it with verve, with a sense of fun almost, pointing me in the direction of a more robust, more romantic sense of what "spirituality" might ultimately be about.

As I think back now, however, I wasn't aware of his Narnia series itself. So here I was, hardly a kid anymore, losing myself inside of these seven little books, beginning with *The Lion, the Witch, and The Wardrobe*. But Narnia and all that happens in it for Lucy and the others—above all, their dealings with the White Witch and with Aslan, the lion, a thinly veiled stand-in for Christ—is not my main concern here. Stuck on this scene of her making her way into the wardrobe and out the other side, my main concern is with the experience of entering worlds other than our supposedly "real world" through the doorway of reading itself, and not just reading fiction alone, but the act of reading, period. So, I'm going to take Lucy's discovery as a launch pad to talk about the reading life and, between the lines, paralleling it, the English life as well.

By this, I mean an idealized English life, frozen somewhere in the 1950s, the kind that only a "colonial" could envision, one brought up in rural Canada on made-in-England Matchbox Toys, Minibrix, and Corgi Cars. I mean a picture-postcard life of rolling green fields, cozy little villages, and sprightly conversation over tea, which authors such as Lewis, though also Graham Greene, Iris Murdoch, Thomas Hardy, and others in their fashion, fleshed out in my imagination and seeded within me the deepest sort of longing for. This same longing led to my plan, following seminary in Toronto, to set sail across the pond, enroll at that other place (Cambridge) and, lured by its dreaming spires, to embark upon my

Ph.D.. Alas, and as I've said already in this book, I never completed it, indeed barely started it, bailing out of the program in under ten months to my enduring shame. To this day, it remains an unfinished chapter in the story of my life, a chapter I've returned to repeatedly in my dreams, hoping to work out a more satisfying conclusion. But, of course, you can't talk about reading without talking about books, which constitute the one recurring theme throughout my life as a whole.

Books—reading them and, as it turns out, writing them, too—have basically *become* my life. My home is filled with them, of all types on all topics, and I wouldn't have it otherwise. "A good book," I read once, "is the lifeblood of a precious spirit." Well, then, I must have a precious spirit indeed! My sister and many of my friends, of course, read books in electronic form alone, on a tablet or a pad, but that's not for me. I need the thing itself, in my hands, and the palpable pleasure of sitting in my favorite chair beneath my favorite lamp, turning the pages, feeling them, smelling them, with a pen or marker handy to highlight passages that, for whatever odd reasons, set my mind spinning. And out of some obscure brand of OCD, I make my own index at the back of the book to keep track of which passages speak to me the most, so that I can return to them later, often finding that the me for whom a given passage was so meaningful initially has morphed into a me who finds a deeper or a different meaning further on.

It's as if the book lives on inside of me, its significance accruing quietly with time. In some dim corner of my mind, interacting in an alchemical manner with my own memories and emotions, as in a compost heap, it has a life all its own. It's only with the greatest difficulty, therefore, that I can part with it. For I never know what fresh meaning it might hold for me, how it might claim me and quicken me, whenever I pick it up again. Its meanings, like those of my more poignant memories, develop gradually and magically inside of me. They thicken up. They grow. Indeed, I have relationships with books that have grown more deeply and lasted lots longer than my relationships with many of my dearest friends.

Of course, I have books that I've never read at all, and at this stage most likely never will, books that I bought or borrowed believing there was something in them that, at some point, I needed to know, to understand, to feel. Sadly, in the next round of downsizing to which I periodically subject myself, some of them I will at last let go of altogether. Not because I've outgrown them or think that I'm above them, but for the sheer practicality of not having so many bloody boxes of them to lug—again—from A to B. The general rule, though, is to hang onto them for as long as I can, until the day comes that I have matured enough, had my horizons stretched enough, or gone through the requisite life experiences to act as receptors for whatever gifts they may have to give. When the reader is ready, the book will have already arrived.

No, letting go of books is not easy, for a book is far from just a thing to me. It is a doorway into another world, a world of knowledge or theory, of insight or imagination. It is an opening into a realm of ideas, of experiences, of feelings that I can gain access to in scarcely any other way. Of course, no book, nor our experience of reading it, can hold a candle, many would argue, to Real Life, to raw, unfiltered Experience. But such experience, I would argue back, is in fact shaped, is extended and intensified—its meaning is revealed—in proportion to the extent and intensity of our reading life itself.

What little Lucy felt in worming her way through the wardrobe and out the other side—the curiosity, the expectation, the wondering what's next—is what I feel in picking up a book for the first time. There's something in this for me, I think to myself, bookworm that I am—an insight, an idea, a question, a concept, a quote, a discovery, a unique take on Life. Otherwise, I wouldn't have been pulled to it in the first place, and then kept it, as the case can be, for decades on end. There's something in it that my mind, my soul, my psyche, or whatever you care to call it, knows that it needs in order to open it out to the next level of awareness, of understanding. I read it, as Annie Dillard offers in her little book *The Writing Life*, "in hope of beauty laid bare, life heightened and its deepest mystery probed." In short, reading is an adventure.

Chapter after chapter, book after book, Lucy and the others go on to have many an adventure in the land of Narnia, which is also why I identify so sharply with that initial scene, for adventure was what I grew up adoring, or at least the vicarious adventure I could partake in through reading. Certainly the books that I feasted on earlier in my life were very much of that variety, whether the adventures of the Bobbsey Twins, the Hardy Boys, or Nancy Drew, or of Lightfoot the Deer, Chatterer the Red Squirrel, and other denizens of the forest that author Thornton W. Burgess brought so delightfully to life. While they provided a welcome escape from certain less than pleasant aspects of my home environment and helped me while away the time during those long boring hours when, as a somewhat sickly kid, I had to stay at home from school, they also seeded in me—the child that books built—the sunny assumption that, all things considered, Life itself is not a tragedy, nor a farce, but an adventure. Indeed, I've kept returning to this one key theme across the years. With an assortment of books that I have on my shelves, the word "adventure" is central to their titles, among them *The Adventure of Living*, *The Cosmic Adventure*, *Adventures of Ideas*, and *Adventure Inward*, plus one or two take-offs on the fairy tale genre itself in a series called *Choose Your Own Adventure*.

The entire topic of "narrative" that has focused my mind for nearly forty years has also been one vast adventure, the one thing—if there is one thing—that I was put here to pursue: an adventure of ideas par excellence. Within that adventure, which found me as much as I found it, I view life-story work—of the sort, for instance, that the three of us have been doing in this book—as an adventure in itself. It is an adventure inward, an adventure of self-exploration, self-discovery, and self-creation all in one. Indeed, I've developed a little workshop that I've regularly given in recent years called *The Autobiographical Adventure: Exploring the Stories of Our Lives*, the majority of those attending it being older adults.

More to the point, I've come to view aging itself as an adventure—not a sick joke played on us by a cold, indifferent universe, but an adventure which, somewhere around the latter end of so-called midlife, we enter into through a doorway. It is an adventure fraught, like any undertaking worthy of the word, with all manner of twists and turns, of villains and adversities, and of obstacles, outer and inner, to be faced. But it is fraught, as well, with lessons to learn, discoveries to make, and wisdom to share. It is potentially a way not to the darkness but to the light, where entirely new perspectives on our lives can start coming into view, including new perspectives on the destination toward which the adventure is leading.

I speak of Death, which in spite of the materialistic-scientistic spirit that dominates our times, I refuse to envision as intrinsically tragic, as The End in any ultimate sense. Sitting in her London flat, writing in her journal, Florida Scott-Maxwell reflects back on past pregnancies when "the child seemed to claim almost all my body, my strength, my breath." "Is life a pregnancy?" she asks herself rhetorically, then "that would make death a birth." Not a termination, but a transition. Not a dead end but a doorway into … what? More life, Other Lives, The Other Side, The Great Adventure?

Here, again, I draw on the thoughts of Teilhard de Chardin—a man of science to the core and yet, as a Jesuit priest, of the most heightened spirituality, a mystic even, for whom Science and Religion are not antagonistic endeavors but complementary at heart. In his vision of the cosmos, the spiritual and material are intertwined in one vast, evolutionary unfolding, an inherently purposeful, meaningful process in which, ironically, death itself plays a pivotal role. He laces his moving book, *Hymn of the Universe*, with enticing phrases like "the mystery hidden in the womb of death." Indeed, death, he writes, is "organically necessary if the divine fire is to descend upon us" and, through it, we will be "falling back ... into the cosmic forces." Death, he says, causes "us to lose our footing completely in ourselves so as to deliver us over to the powers of heaven and earth." Death "surrenders us completely to God; ... makes us pass into God."

The vision coursing through such lofty language, while surely not everyone's cup of tea, parallels the one that fueled Lewis himself, though he articulates his version of it in an ever-so-English (if not boyish) and certainly more narrative a manner. In the last paragraph of *The Last Battle*, the final volume in the Narnia series, after Aslan has broken the news to Lucy and her siblings that they, in fact, died in a train accident and are, thus, "as you used to call it in the Shadow-lands—dead," Lewis, the master raconteur, winds up his grand tale with words geared to stir the hearts of children everywhere, young and old alike—my own heart included:

> ... the things that began to happen to them after that were so great and beautiful that I cannot write them. And for us this is the end of all the stories, and we can most truly say that they all lived happily ever after. But for them it was only the beginning of the real story. All their life in this world and all their adventures in Narnia had only been the cover and the title page: now at last they were beginning Chapter One of The Great Story, which no one on earth has read: which goes on forever: in which every chapter is better than the one before.

A few years before *The Lion, The Witch, and The Wardrobe* first appeared, Lewis published an essay in which he quibbled with the idea of designating a particular class of books as "children's books." With characteristic candor, he dismissed it as "silly." Apart from books of information, he went on, "no book is really worth reading at the age of ten which is not equally (and often far more) worth reading at the age of fifty," a philosophy that he himself adhered to in regularly rereading childhood favorites like *The Wind in the Willows* and the books of Beatrix Potter. Revisiting Lewis' book at seventy, I can scarcely disagree. I've gotten more out of it, and read more into it, than I could possibly have done in my twenties. And it's precisely the intervening years that make the difference. While a big part of me wishes I could have those years back, or some of them at least, the larger part is thankful for the layers of Life that they've laid down inside me—the good and the bad, the bitter and the sweet, the adventures and misadventures alike. I bless the perspective that all of this has afforded me and, even more, the heart of wonder which, like that of little Lucy, pushing through the wardrobe, it's made beat all the faster.

PART III

On To Your Own Adventure

CHAPTER 19

The Parabolic Power of the Second Half of Life: A Few Further Reflections

Wonder, discovery, adventure: these are the watchwords of that intricate inner journey of the second half of life. And it is a journey in which stories themselves—from the get-go, our main means of making meaning—play a pivotal role.

As these little tales we've been exploring have done for each of us, stories have the power to shape our values and our views in the profoundest of ways. From those that our parents may have read to us as children, to the movies we've been moved by every time we watch them, to the dramas, TV shows, and novels that we've revisited across the years, stories can speak to us so deeply that it's as if they worm their way straight into our hearts, whether for better or for worse. On the negative side, in other words, stories can inspire us in not always life-affirming ways. It is possible to be caught in the grips of dark, depressive, dysfunctional narratives that limit our lives and stifle our souls, or our families, in countless sad ways, which is why we'll probably always need therapists and analysts (like Barbara herself once was) to help us "re-story" in healthier directions. On the positive side, though, stories can offer us avenues to a wisdom, if not to Truth, that is inaccessible by any other means. Not truth in terms of tidy answers to life's perennial questions, but something more organic and dynamic: truth, you might say, that questions our answers as much as the other way around.

Given such power, stories of almost any kind can serve, therefore, as *parables*: as narratives that open our minds to novel ways of see-ing. Even those tales whose moral is explicitly spelled out ("slow but steady wins the race") can, when probed a wee bit further, open up new levels of awareness concerning the stories of our own lives. It's as if the one story addresses the other, interrogating it, illuminating it, enriching it.

The stories of our own lives have the same sort of parabolic poten-tial. Reflecting on them closely, especially those that we've held onto, unwittingly, as somehow central to our sense of self—our signature stories, if you like (and we've sprinkled this book with a few of our own)—can lead to a heightened understanding of our greatest hopes and deepest fears. This makes it critical, then, not just to tell our stories but to listen to what our stories tell us. Put another way, it is in the complex, meandering, many-layered *novel* that we've been quietly composing all our life and which, in our memory and imagination is synonymous *with* "our life," that we find our own unique truth.

In facing the challenges—physical, emotional, social, and more—that come with the second half of life, we therefore face a choice at every stage. We can approach aging as a way to the darkness or a way to the light. We can view it, and live it, as a tragedy of slowly, sadly *getting* old—which, alas, is the view to which the formal study of aging too frequently defaults, focusing as it does on the outside of aging and leaving the intricate, ever-shifting inside all but ig-nored. Or, regardless of the negatives that aging invariably involves, perhaps even because of them, we can embrace it as an adventure of consciously and creatively *growing* old.

Whatever our choice, aging presents us with its own set of developmental tasks that are every bit as critical to tackle as walking or talking or tying our shoes. But they are far subtler and more internal in nature. They are autobiographical tasks at base, and therefore narrative tasks as well. They concern less the landscape of action that a story is said to possess, a life story included, than the landscape of consciousness: the realm not of action and events but of understanding and interpretations. Together, they concern what's been called the "philosophic homework" of later life. That work has to do, among other things, with pondering the memories—or more accurately the *stories*, for that's what memories mostly are, autobiographical memories, that is—which we've most equated with what "our life" has been and who, therefore, "we" are. It has to do with expanding and examining those stories to some degree of depth: stories that, siren-like, can beckon to us more urgently with time.

Among the tasks this work entails—this *storywork*, as you might think of it—is dealing with unfinished business in our relationships with others, living or dead; in other words, owning up to grudges or regrets that we've held onto, or fences that need mending, or things we've left unsaid. Entailed as well is reconnecting with interests and talents that, in making our way in the world, we've left to one side. Entailed, too, is assimilating into our life narrative events that have resisted easy understanding: troubling, traumatic, or otherwise negative experiences within which, ideally, we can find some measure of redemption, can retrieve some treasured insight, some hard-earned lesson. Overall, what's entailed is cultivating *a good strong story* to live by, and age by: a story that's flexible and expansive, open and thick, a story that breathes. In short, the work of later life is about engaging in what psychologists of aging call Life Review, something that's deemed essential to achieving a measure of inner integrity as we age. It's about stepping back from the minutiae of our lives, the ins and outs of our journey through time, and, figuratively speaking, pulling ourselves together. It's about *re-membering* our lives, about reconnecting their various components. It's about savoring the still-unfolding novel of our lives in all its complexity and depth, and mining its endless potential for meaning.

At bottom, the three of us are convinced, aging is not reducible to a collection of deficits and declines. These concern the outside of aging primarily, not necessarily the inside. No, amid its many less than pleasant features, again perhaps even *because* of them, aging invites us to turn inward and to embark on a heightened search for meaning, which makes it an intrinsically "spiritual" endeavor, where that word is interpreted in the broadest of terms. What is the meaning, aging nudges us to ask, not just of Life in general, but of My Life in particular? What is my unique legacy, my unique story? What difference, if any, have I made in the world? And what, if anything, is my destiny beyond it?

For many of us, our experience of spirituality has been shaped by a particular religion, replete with its rituals and creeds and its overarching story of the world, and with the built-in answers it provides us as to where we have come from, why we are here, and where we are bound. For some of us, happily, that tradition (and the grand narrative that goes with it) has been more or less open and affirming, and filled with astonishing resources, such as stories and symbols, hymns and myths, to help us make sense of the vagaries of our lives and our world. It's afforded us room to maneuver as the plot of our life thickens, plus a perspective for viewing its ups and downs, its pleasures and pains, with a humble blend of irony and affection. For others of us, however, the ideology we've adhered to and the narrative it espouses is a rigid, imprisoning structure that allows us scant freedom to take it on our own terms, to question and critique it. Its message is: All or Nothing, Right or Wrong, Our Way or The Highway. It therefore fosters not growth, not narrative development, not narrative openness, but narrative foreclosure.

By strictly prescribing the plot by which we should live, with few substitutes permitted, it shuts our own stories down.

Here's where the power of story itself enters in its liberating power, its *parabolic* power. Parables, like those that Jesus told, or those of the Sufi masters, can serve as counter-stories: stories which undermine the hold of larger narratives that can stunt our development in a multitude of ways. Chief among such narratives, of course, is the narrative of *decline* that dominates our society today, as far as later life is concerned, casting aging itself as a villain to defeat and an aging population less as a resource to be cherished than as a problem to be solved. Guided by this narrative, the formal study of aging (as both Andy and Bill can attest) has become so focused on, for instance, the mechanics of aging—on the toll that it takes on our bodies and brains—that the *meaning* of aging, or the meaning *in* aging, is virtually eclipsed, as is any notion that aging might be the sort of intriguing, internal adventure we've been envisioning in this book. The same narrative can infect our individual experience of aging as well, blinding us to its positive possibilities, to the clarity and maturity and enlargement of soul that, if we let it, it can bring. Instead, we view aging as a downward drift to decrepitude and death, with little by way of significance in itself: not as, potentially, the fulfillment of the life cycle but its depressing denouement.

As we hope has become clearer for you in making your way through this book, *any* story—no matter how childish it seems on the surface—can serve as a counter-story. Depending on how deeply we let it address us, it can transform our lives, or at least our *view* of our lives, which in the end is the key. While we can't change the events of our lives (what happened, happened, and that's that), we can change how we understand them, how we *story* them. And it's our story of them that makes all the difference. The tales that we've reflected on here have obviously had this kind of impact for us, as they may have had for you as well. They possess this marvelous quality of transcending time. We can get as much out of them at sixty or seventy as we did at sixteen or six, and frequently far more, for our horizon of understanding has grown that much wider. We can see more in them. An assortment of metaphors leap to mind to capture how this happens.

Given the rich (if not always happy) array of experiences that we've garnered along life's path, plus the benefits that hindsight presumably affords us, these stories serve as mirrors in which we can glimpse ourselves reflected back, however distorted the image might be. They serve as sieves for filtering a lifetime of memories, straining out whatever gems of insight, whatever questions or themes, might be hidden in the mix. And they serve as blank screens onto which we can project whatever hopes and hurts, fantasies and fears, have been coursing through our hearts since our earliest days. They thus have this knack of crawling under our skin and tapping into the oddities and complexities of our inner world, so much so that we can't stop thinking about them. Or rather, we can't stop thinking *through* them, since they can illuminate those complexities with a fresh and frequently comical light. Conveniently, we become more attuned to such complexities anyway, given a capacity that psychologists have said we tend to develop naturally with age. It's the capacity to see the forest for the trees; to accept the Yin and the Yang of life; to appreciate the meanings in metaphors and the nuances in stories that would have eluded us in our younger years; and, in general, to look at situations and people—ourselves included—from a variety of angles.

The knack that we're talking about, the knack of remaining in our minds across the years, is the same one that any great story possesses. Just ask the members of the book club you belong to, where you're reading and discussing, say, a classic work of fiction. The book has an ending, to be sure, but there's no end whatever to the meanings you can pull from it, the discoveries you can make, the development—the *narrative* development—it can deepen in your respective lives. Nor is there any need to arrive at conclusions concerning it, for the closure you experience in reading it is less a closed kind of closure, less a *fore*-closure, with all questions answered and all loose ends tied together, than an *open* closure, with loads of themes to keep considering.

The little tales that we've delved into here have been for us this very type of stories, even if some of them have a happy-ever-after kind of ending. Happy endings or not, however, they are still amazingly open texts. Their meanings are anything but predetermined. And they have inspired in us all manner of reflections as we've played with their significance for our own lives. They've stirred up the soil of our lives, aerating it, opening us (and you, too, hopefully) to fresh ways of thinking and feeling, fresh questions and insights. For, however simple they might seem at first glance, the more that we've crawled inside of them (or let them crawl inside of us), the more we've appreciated the themes that they convey and the possibilities they allow for deepened understanding—of ourselves as aging individuals and of aging itself.

Because of how they've haunted us ever since we first encountered them, the tales that we've looked into in this book can serve, therefore (here comes another metaphor!), as Rorschach blots for the inner workings of our psyches. Into their plots and themes, and into their characters, which often are archetypes for aspects of our own personalities, we can read whatever issues might still be pressing on our minds, issues that have woven themselves into the slow questions that have formed inside of us across the intervening years—questions that are unique, in many ways, to us alone. We interpret these stories, we discern their significance, through the lens of the stories of our own life. But the reverse is true as well. In reading them after all this time, they turn out not at all to be childish things that we ought, at last, to put away, to grow out of. Quite the contrary. They possess this uncanny capacity—this wisdom, you could say—to interpret us, to illuminate aspects of our characters and to light up corners of our past that would otherwise lurk in the dark; to reveal patterns in our experience and our world that linger at the edges of our field of view. In short, they read us as much as we read them. This is the glorious power that stories so often possess, their parabolic power, and it is why we can't survive for long in a world without them—assuming such a world exists.

So then ... how you might go about connecting stories to your own lives, what sorts of strategies and steps you might employ in doing so, and what kinds of questions you might ask, this is (last but by no means least) the topic that we turn to next.

CHAPTER 20

New Meanings From Old Tales:
An Invitation

Throughout this book, we've been looking at a motley collection of stories that have stuck with us since childhood, though we could easily have looked at two or three times as many. The fact that we remembered these ones in particular, though, speaks to the strength of their effect on us as we were growing up. To some extent, we have been able to recover our initial and very visceral reactions to them. However, we are viewing them now through the lens of greater intellectual, emotional, and spiritual maturity overall, which means that, ideally, we're in a position to respond to them with a deeper, fuller appreciation of what they have to offer us.

Stories stir us in different ways. Some immediately stun us. Some appeal to us at the outset yet require a bit of focused attention, slowly showing us connections that aren't immediately evident. And then there are others, perhaps those that are most personally meaningful, which require significant effort to unpack. Ultimately, though, they can prove extremely illuminating, yielding the fruit of greater self-knowledge as we come to recognize within them aspects of our lives that we've avoided facing up to hitherto.

One of the best indicators that a story has something to teach us is simply that we recall it. New stories, too, of course, can shed light on dimensions of our lives that are worth attending to. But those tales that we come back to year after year seem to call to us with particular force. Which stories stand out for *you*? Why? Which ones are most intriguing? Which ones delight you? Scare you? Offend you? How might each of them speak to you now in fresh new ways?

The purpose of this chapter—a kind of appendix, if you will—is to encourage you to take a personal look at stories that have caught your own attention and kept it across the years. The approach we have in mind is not an academic exercise, or even a primarily intellectual one. Rather, we're suggesting that you delve into, so to speak, your *relationship* with each such tale. The questions we are posing here are thus meant merely as jumping-off points that may (or may not) lead you to a deepened understanding of yourself or of other important figures in your life, an understanding that, conveniently, age itself can naturally bring with it. As we move into later life, that is, we have the gift of all the years that have passed and that we can pore over and ponder—all the experiences we've cherished, the joys we've known, the people we've loved, as well as all the choices we've made, which have led us down paths of fulfillment and discovery. But we can look back, too, on the difficulties in our lives—the losses, the cruelties, the disappointments, and the suffering, both physical and emotional. Though, true, it can be painful to examine our flaws and our limitations, we have the great advantage over younger people of having come through a lot, which means that if we haven't always conquered, we have at least survived. So, we needn't fear an honest appraisal of our failures as well as our successes.

The use of familiar stories in the way we've been doing in this book may become part of the life review that many of us are wont to undertake with age, as we try to figure out and come to terms with our past, our present, and our future alike. And it can be an interesting way, too, of reminding us that our lives are not limited to one single narrative, but involve different relationships and events, different challenges and gifts. The proverbial "story of my life" is not just one coherent account, in other words. Instead, multiple subplots, storylines, and strands have formed us into the complex creatures that we are.

There are many approaches to the sort of story investigation on which we're inviting you to embark. One of the main ones, though, is to loosen the ties to literalism and relax into the realm of metaphor. Although in your daily life a walk is just a walk, a walk taken by a character in a fairy tale invites you to see your own life as a journey, one that is wide-ranging in scope and filled with sometimes surprising elements that are unique to you. In short, we're asking you to inhabit the world of the story, to melt into it in ways that help you see yourself and your past—as well as your present and your future—with clarity and, in the end (we hope), joy.

We are always free to take great liberties in playing with what stories say to us, even to discard limitations in them that initially seemed essential. For example, in the approach we've been taking in this book, we're not necessarily bound by the gender or age assignment of characters. The oldest son could well be a character to whom a younger daughter might relate, depending on family structure and values. A woman who knows what it is to take responsibility for others might well identify with a story's king. Many of us might relate to someone who is asleep for years, only finding herself by a surprise awakening from an outside source. Life in your workplace might well be recognizable, in the story, as life in the palace.

One of our suggestions is that you try to discard assumptions about surface categories and seek connections beneath the surface. In this spirit, we also encourage you to open yourself to multifaceted, even self-contradictory responses. For example, you may be the young girl aching for the prince to discover her and release her from the bonds of poverty, or sleep, or whatever else is hindering her full development. Yet, in the same story, you also may be the prince, noticing the beauty that others don't see, finding the elusive element that will make your life complete. You may be the despised and denigrated one, and you may also be the entitled one whose public stature, though welcome, is unearned. It is not essential here to harmonize the different aspects of your life situation, your gifts and limitations, your fears and desires. Rather, it may be fun, not to mention, thought-provoking, to acknowledge and accept the variety you embody—all of which has played, and continues to play, an important role in who you are.

FIVE CORE QUESTIONS TO ASK

One way to use stories as jumping-off points for personal reflection is to set aside time on a regular basis to take a fresh look at those you remember from your life, or to take a book of fairy tales or other stories and visit them anew. First, read the story. Spend some time—five to fifteen minutes, maybe—reviewing the story mentally: recalling its plot, the flow of its action, and its most notable aspects overall. You might want to jot down your recollection of the main parts of the story. As you look at the areas of interest and the questions, take whatever time you need. You may want to journal some of your responses, and continue thinking about memories, issues, and feelings that have been evoked. Don't rush here. The point is to engage your memory, your emotions, and your thoughts to see what the story has to tell you at this point in your life. After you have done this, set it aside. Be available for further thoughts and reflections in the week or so following.

We need not look at every aspect of a story, or even at all of the apparent themes in it. Perhaps a deeper look at one aspect will lead you to a recollection or a reverie that could engross you for an afternoon, or even an entire day. If you choose to spend hours of contented daydreaming and remembering, with no particular constructive focus, it is all to the good. These are not exam questions on a test with a time limit; they are invitations to reflection and self-connection—to re-membering—that can illuminate your past and deepen your sense of yourself these many years later.

To take a story and examine our life through it, one approach is to look at five core components: (1) our emotional response to the story; (2) the scene; (3) the characters; (4) the plot; and (5) the meaning that the story has for us. Many stories can be applicable to our lives: some immediately stun or delight or offend us; some, with greater attention, can bring to mind aspects of ourselves that, unwittingly or otherwise, we have avoided examining. A closer look at each of these elements can help us delve into the personal significance it may have for us.

First of all, when you recall the story, *what do you feel?* Do you rejoice with the formerly downtrodden princess? Do you happily sneer at the evil sisters? Are you drawn to the scene with the fairy godmother, delighting in the beautiful gown and lovely shoes? Do you identify with the fear of the lost children? The rage of Rumpelstiltskin? What other feelings are conjured up?

Sometimes our feelings are those of warm delight: the characters in the story are clever, strong, and honorable, and they are rightly rewarded for their virtues. This is the way the world should work, and we feel relieved and glad that, here at least, it does so. What might this say about our view of ourselves, or of what we want to be like? Does this speak to a worldview in which, ultimately, all is well? Might this be connected to our spiritual or religious life and to our view of the ultimate nature of the universe? And, if so, what role, if any, are we to play? How are we doing? Are there ways to maximize our joy, our sense of gratitude and peace?

At times, some of the feelings evoked by these stories—for instance, pleasure at another's (even if deserved!) misery; relief at being rid of an unpleasant person, etc.—could be uncomfortable, and we might not want to admit them. It's just a story, though, and so no one is requiring us to write down the most unappealing aspects of our own nature.

That said, it could be worthwhile to acknowledge that such feelings are nonetheless part of our personality, no matter how much we strive to have others (and even ourselves) see us in a more ideal light. The evil stepmother is a trope, not just because in the times such stories were probably developed, pregnancy and childbirth were relatively frequent causes of death, but because it is so common for people to be disliked by others, often through no fault of their own. And it is often the case that we ourselves do and say—or at least think—unlikable things, and can, on occasion, be downright unpleasant.

It can be valuable to recognize those unpleasant aspects of ourselves, not necessarily to change them, but at least to acknowledge our role in, for instance, certain tense relationships in our lives. It is true that, though many of the "evil" stepmothers in such stories show no particular sign of being evil, replacing a mother is a tough job, and very few of us, stepmother or no, are always at our best. Which situations make us most angry or miserable, mean-spirited, and unlikeable? Has this changed over the years? Would it be useful to consider ways of limiting our exposure to things in real life that bring out the worst in us?

Second, *what is the setting?* When and where does the story take place? Is it set in pre-industrial times, in the countryside somewhere, alongside a river, or in a palace? Is it about a family, with little children? A kingdom, with attendants and royalty? An American southern plantation? An alternate fantasyland ruled by a giant or peopled with strange or endearing creatures? You may want to spend a bit of time thinking about the effect that physical environments have on you, the ways they have shaped you, strengthened you, limited you. In what ways were certain of them like the environment of the story? Is the setting Edenic, simple, lovely? Or are people poor, struggling to find enough to eat? Is there a war going on?

How do you relate to the setting? Were you raised on a farm? In a city? A suburb? Was your family's social life reminiscent in any way of the social life depicted in the story? Idyllic pleasures—maybe until some tragedy interrupted it? Internecine warfare? Poor people at the mercy of rich ones? With which do you identify? What reactions do you have to the setting? Does it seem nostalgically appealing? Do you see yourself and your early family life represented at all in it? Do you wish you had grown up in such a place? Are you delighted that you didn't?

Third, *who are the characters?* Parents, children, good godmothers, evil godmothers, princes, princesses, kings, queens, traveling salesmen, farmworkers, personality-rich animals? How might your family of origin—or the family that you later chose or created, or your work "home" or some other community—be seen in these characters? Do you identify with Sleeping Beauty? With the king, or the giant? Do the members of either your family of origin or the one you've chosen or created as an adult have any similarity to the characters in the story? An older brother can at times be experienced like an evil king—and like a little sister at others!

Many of us choose—consciously or otherwise—to replicate familial roles in our adult life: being the charming, well-liked (and sometimes surprisingly competent) "little brother" of the group, or the reconciler of conflicts in the family, at the office, or among friends, for instance. Others of us take on a role as an adult that is very different from the one we had in our family of origin. Whom do you recognize in this tale? Whom do you wish had been part of the family? Where do you see yourself? Is it a comfortable role?

Do you see Little Red Riding Hood and think, "Oh, I can just imagine *being* her—I love to visit sick people, take them food, and visit with them. And I can well imagine chatting with the wolf and then delighting in finding some flowers to take to my grandmother. I'd be enjoying a leisurely afternoon, and would be so glad to see Grandma, even if she did seem a bit off. Being ill can do that." Or is Little Red Riding Hood definitely *not* your sort? "If I had a job to do," you might say, "I'd put on my little red coat, focus on the task, and do it. I wouldn't stop and waste time talking to a stranger, and I certainly wouldn't wander into a field of wildflowers and start frolicking among the violets. I would take the plate Mother had prepared, go straight to Grandma's, and give her the food. Chat a bit, and end of story. The wolf wouldn't have had time to barge in with his evil, and everything would have been fine."

Fourth, *what is the plot* of the story, and how do you relate to it? Are you in any way Cinderella, plucked from poor obscurity and entering the realm of royalty? Do you wish you were? Did you imagine great riches and power when you started your career, and did you—or did you not—receive them? Either way, do you—and is it reasonable to—attribute that result to your own hard work, or lack thereof, or to chance? Are you ever the dreadful stepsister, jealous and mean-spirited? If so, can you empathize with the assumptions that she made about her own worthiness, and the terrible defeat she suffered through no change in herself? Have you ever—or are you now—wandering like Hansel and Gretel through a forest with no clear sense of where to go, or of what's ahead? It is very likely that any story which appeals to you—or which stands out in your memory even if it is *not* appealing—speaks to an experience or situation that is meaningful to you in some way. What connections do you see?

One of the questions raised when talking about the plot of a story is the degree to which we have contributed to our current situation. Clearly, in numerous stories, the characters are innocent of the disasters that befall them. Equally, characters often have no part in the wondrous fortune that is given them. From time to time, though, and often in surprising ways, characters are able to make huge changes in their lives. Looking at our current situation—and at the major undertakings of our lives—how much has been due solely, or even primarily, to our own actions? How much has been the result of the situation into which we were born, or with which we were provided before we had any real agency? And how much has been due to our own autonomy? How have the events of our lives shaped us, and how do they continue to rule our lives? Are there any current life situations that affect us negatively? Do we want to explore the possibility of making any changes?

Fifth, and finally, *what does the story mean to us*? This component of exploring a story asks whether there are larger issues that are either involved in it or implied by it that inform or challenge our worldview, our belief system, our values, our sense of spirituality. For example, in probably the majority of our well-known tales, the "happy ending" is a presentation of a moral victory, made possible by a combination of the active—but ultimately futile—cruelty of those who lose out and the herculean efforts of the morally upright heroines and heroes.

Perhaps there are other spiritual issues involved here, connected not just to morality but, say, to the presence, power, and generosity of love. A focus on the evil stepsisters, and their own limitations and dissatisfactions, could lead us to a shift toward a greater empathy for others, and also for ourselves. We might wonder about the spiritual implications of societies based on zero-sum competition for limited resources, rather than on cooperation in sharing those resources.

What might the story mean, not just to our view of the world, but to our behavior in that world? Might our search for meaning, prompted and perhaps guided by the story, invite us to make changes in our attitudes, actions, or relationships? If so, what sorts of changes?

Surely one aspect of our spirituality that is frequently engaged in such stories is the connection between the spiritual life and our material life here on earth. In what realm do we exist? Both? What is the intersection of the spiritual and the material? When the stories speak of "happily ever after," for example, what do we think about our future after death? What existence, if any, is there after death? What beliefs, or hopes, or fears does that question engender in us? Can we perhaps enter the "happily ever after" now, before we die?

MOVING FORWARD

In this final chapter, and more broadly in the book as a whole, we have suggested an approach to connecting with your lives that can be undertaken individually. Setting aside time for reflection, and journaling about some of your thoughts, feelings, and connections, could be quite healing, revelatory even. And doing so on a regular, scheduled basis could become a meaningful part of your personal, inner journey. But, in addition, or as an alternative, you might consider getting together on a regular basis with a few others in your circle who are interested in self-reflective discussions of the deeper meanings that are embedded in old tales. Such a group might form what Bill and his colleague, Gary Kenyon, call a "wisdom environment." It might meet monthly, for example, to look at how each of you hears and responds to a specific story. However you do it, an ongoing contemplation of the personal significance of old totemic tales could enrich your understanding of the unique journey—the distinctive adventure—that is your life.

References and Resources

At the beginning of many chapters in this book are summaries of the stories that we've reflected on within them. In composing these summaries, we've drawn from folklorists, translators, and other experts who, thankfully, have assembled particular collections of tales. We wish to honor their important work here.

As regards Mother Goose tales (e.g., *Little Red Riding Hood*), this means Charles Perrault. For Grimm's Fairy Tales (e.g., *Hansel and Gretel, Sleeping Beauty, The Fisherman and His Wife*), it means F. J. Olcott, while for Hans Christian Andersen's stories (e.g., *The Emperor's New Clothes, The Ugly Duckling, What The Old Man Does is Always Right*), it is J. H. Stickney. The work of J. Jacobs was our source for English fairy tales (e.g., *Jack and The Beanstalk*); that of G. F. Townsend and L. Gibbs for Aesop's fables (e.g., *The Tortoise and The Hare, The Horse, The Ox, and The Man*); and of Joel Chandler Harris for *Br'er Rabbit and Tar Baby*.

Concerning stories from the Bible (*Jesus Calms the Storm, The Prodigal Son, The Rich Young Ruler*), we've drawn on whatever version we're most familiar with, whether the King James Version or the New Revised Standard Version, and so on. With only two stories we've reflected on—*Jam Yesterday, Jam Tomorrow, But Never Jam Today*, and *The Lion, The Witch, and The Wardrobe*—do we quote directly from the original authors: Lewis Carroll and C. S. Lewis, respectively. With these sources in mind, plus others that have informed us or inspired us along the way, we offer the following list.

Andersen, H. C. (2008). *Fairy tales of Hans Christian Andersen*. [Project Gutenberg 27200].

Atkinson, R. (1995). *The gift of stories: Practical and spiritual applications of autobiography, life stories, and personal mythmaking*. Bergin & Garvey.

Baldwin, C. (2005). *Storycatcher: Making sense of our lives through the power and practice of story*. New World Library.

Bettelheim, B. (1989). *The uses of enchantment: The meaning and importance of fairy tales*. Vintage.

Booker, C. (2004). *The seven basic plots: Why we tell stories*. Continuum.

Booth, W. (1992). *The art of growing older: Writers on living and aging*. University of Chicago Press.

Campbell, J., & Moyers, B. (1988). *The power of myth*. Doubleday.

Carroll, L. (1976). Through the looking-glass and what Alice found there. *The complete works of Lewis Carroll*. Random House. (Original work published 1871).

Chinen, A. (2002). *In the ever after: Fairy tales and the second half of life*. Chiron.

Cohen, G. (2005). *The mature mind: The positive power of the aging brain*. Basic Books.

de Chardin, P. T. (1970). *Hymn of the universe*. Fountain.

de Medeiros, K. (2013). *Narrative gerontology in research and practice*. Springer.

Erikson, E., Erikson, J., & Kivnick, H. (1986). *Vital involvement in old age*. W. W. Norton.

Freeman, M. (2010). *Hindsight: The promise and peril of looking backward*. Oxford University Press.

Gibbs, L. (Trans.). (2008). *Aesop's fables* (No. 237). Oxford University Press.

Hampl, P. (1999). *I could tell you stories: Sojourns in the land of memory*. W. W. Norton.

Harris, J. C. (1881). *Uncle Remus: His songs and his sayings*. [Project Gutenberg 2306]

Hayflick, L. (1994). *How and why we age*. Ballantine.

Jacobs, J. (Ed.). (1890). *English fairy tales*. David Nutt. [Project Gutenberg 7439]

Kenyon, G., Bohlmeijer, E., & Randall, W. (Eds.) (2011). *Storying later life: Issues, investigations, and interventions in narrative gerontology*. Oxford University Press.

Kenyon, G., & Randall, W. (1997). *Restorying our lives: Personal growth through autobiographical reflection*. Praeger.

Lesser, W. (2002). *Nothing remains the same: Rereading and remembering*. Houghton Mifflin.

Lewis, C. S. (1950). *The lion, the witch, and the wardrobe*. Puffin.

Lewis, C. S. (1956). *The last battle*. Puffin.

Moore, T. (2017). *The ageless soul*. St. Martin's.

Nouwen, H., & Gaffney, W. (1976). *Aging: The fulfillment of life*. Anchor.

Olcott, F. J. (Ed.). (1922). *Grimm's fairy tales*. Penn Publishing Company. [Project Gutenberg 52521].

Orsborn, C. (2021). *The making of an old soul: Aging as the fulfillment of life's promise*. White River Press.

Pearson, C. (1989). *The hero within: Six archetypes we live by*. Harper & Row.

Perrault, C. (1901). *The tales of Mother Goose* (C. Welsh, Trans.). D. C. Heath. [Project Gutenberg 17208]. (Original work published 1696)

Randall, W. (2021). The end of the story? Narrative openness in life and death. *Narrative Works*, *9*(2). 152-170.

Randall, W., & Kenyon, G. M. (2001). *Ordinary wisdom: Biographical aging and the journey of life.* Praeger.

Randall, W., & McKim, A. E. (2008). *Reading our lives: The poetics of growing old.* Oxford University Press.

Ruffing, J. (2011). *To tell the sacred tale: Spiritual direction and narrative.* Paulist Press.

Schachter-Shalomi, Z., & Miller, R. (1995). *From age-ing to sage-ing: A profound new vision of growing older.* Warner.

Scott-Maxwell, F. (1968). *The measure of my days.* Penguin.

Spufford, F. (2002). *The child that books built: A life in reading.* Metropolitan.

Stickney, J. H. (Ed.). (1914). *Hans Christian Andersen's fairy tales, first series.* Ginn. [Project Gutenberg 32571.]

Townsend, G. F. (Trans.). (1871). *The fables of Aesop.* Routledge. [Project Gutenberg 21].

Acknowledgements

We wish to acknowledge many who served as mentors in imagining and writing this book. Allan Chinen's *In The Ever After: Fairy Tales and the Second Half of Life* was certainly a model for it, but we also took inspiration from reflections on aging by authors such as Thomas Moore, Anne Lamont, Richard Rohr, Henri Nouwen, Florida Scott-Maxwell, Mark Freeman, Carol Orsborn, and Rick Moody. The insights of past masters like Bruno Bettelheim into the power of fairy tales in children's hearts, and Joan and Erik Erikson into the dynamics of personal development in later life, definitely influenced our conversations as well.

We thank our children—Rick Venutolo, Emily Harris, and Laura Schieve Achenbaum—who seemed intrigued as we shared with them bedtime stories that we had treasured when we listened to our own parents. Friends, colleagues, parishioners, patients, students, even total strangers, whether they knew it or not, have also been great sounding boards as we've pondered the wisdom which such stories hold for us now.

We are indebted, too, to the wonderful team we worked with in the final stages of the publication process: specifically, Christy Day for her sharp eye and creativity in designing the cover and interior, David Hogan for his editorial savvy regarding the text itself, Jeremy Avenarius for the website he created for us, and above all Martha Bullen of Bullen Publishing Services for her encouragement and sage advice at every step along the path. To Bill's colleague, Beth McKim, we are further grateful for her observations about the content, and to his sister, Carol Randall, for her eleventh-hour suggestion concerning the cover.

About the Authors

 **William L. (Bill) Randall** is a retired Professor of Gerontology at St. Thomas University (STU) on Canada's Atlantic coast. Brought up in rural New Brunswick, he holds an A.B. from Harvard College, a Th.M. from Princeton Theological Seminary, and M.Div. and Ed.D. degrees from the University of Toronto.

After a ten-year career as a protestant minister with the United Church of Canada (1979-1989), he taught English and Adult Education for four years at Seneca College in Toronto. In 1995, he began a 27 year career at STU where he taught a range of undergraduate courses in gerontology and helped to pioneer a unique approach to the study of aging known as *narrative* gerontology. Narrative gerontology blends insights from the humanities and social sciences to probe the complex dynamics of inner (or biographical) development in later life.

Bill has given keynotes, papers, and workshops on this approach at conferences and universities in Canada, the US, the UK, the Netherlands, the Czech Republic, Germany, Sweden, Denmark, France, and Spain. Co-recipient of the 2009 Theoretical Developments in Social Gerontology Award from the Gerontological Society of America, Bill is founding co-editor of the *Narrative Works* journal, founding organizer of the Narrative Matters international conferences, and author or co-author of over 70 publications on narrative gerontology and related topics, including eight books. Among these are *Reading Our Lives: The Poetics of Growing Old* and

The Narrative Complexity of Ordinary Life: Tales from the Coffee Shop, both published by Oxford University Press.

To learn more about Bill or his publications, please visit www.williamlrandall.com.

Barbara Lewis is a retired psychoanalyst and an Episcopal priest. Always curious about the nature, causes, and meaning of people and life, she majored in Philosophy at Mt. Holyoke College and studied Philosophy at Columbia University.

She found a psychoanalyst who helped her with the underlying psychological questions and conflicts of her life. Barbara became an analyst herself, earning an M.S.W. from Columbia, and a certification from the National Psychological Association for Psychoanalysis. She had a full-time practice of psychoanalysis in New York City for twenty years, focusing on the myriad issues and workings of psychology in human life.

Barbara and her family moved to Pennsylvania, where they lived for ten years. She had a part-time psychoanalytic practice there, and pursued a growing focus on what she saw as the underpinnings of physical/psychological life: the nature and role of the spiritual life. She trained at the Episcopal Cathedral in Philadelphia and became an Episcopal deacon, then studied at Princeton Theological Seminary and graduated with an M.Div. from the General (Episcopal) Seminary in New York City. In 1999, she was ordained to the Episcopal priesthood just prior to moving with her family to Houston, TX. She served as a parish priest there for over fifteen years before retiring.

Barbara still asks questions about human life: what it is, how and why it was created, what purpose(s) it has. She continues to marvel at the challenges, the joys, and the enigmas of human beings.

 **W. Andrew (Andy) Achenbaum,** Ph.D., is a semi-retired professor of history in the Houston, Texas Medical Center's Consortium on Aging. He is married to Barbara Lewis and is the proud father of two daughters and two grandchildren.

Achenbaum earned his B.A. in American Studies at Amherst College, an M.A. at the University of Pennsylvania, and his Ph.D. in history at the University of Michigan. After learning more about the art of teaching at Canisius College and revising the core curriculum at Carnegie Mellon University, Andy served as professor of history and deputy director of the Institute of Gerontology at the University of Michigan and then became the founding dean of the College of Liberal Arts and Social Sciences at the University of Houston.

For half a century Achenbaum has been critically thinking, lecturing and writing about the meanings and experiences of old age in U.S. history. To interpret intriguing late-life continuities and to fight ageism, Andy has elaborated older Americans' roles in reconfiguring an aging nation's political economy, social and trans-generational policies, and (in)visibility in cultural affairs. Turning 75 in good health this year, he finds it a challenge to balance personal and professional opinions about fairy-tale wisdom and soulful aging in a deeply polarized country.

Achenbaum has published six books, co-edited 12 others, and written more than 200 peer-reviewed articles. Routledge will publish his forthcoming book *Safeguarding Social Security for Future Generations*. A recipient of several awards for his work in gerontology, he chaired the National Council of Aging, and served on national, state, and local advisory boards.

To learn more and contact all three authors, visit www.Fairy-TaleWisdom.com.